The Forty Riders

JOHN LADD

A Black Horse Western

ROBERT HALE · LONDON

© John Ladd 2001
First published in Great Britain 2001

ISBN 0 7090 6892 1

Robert Hale Limited
Clerkenwell House
Clerkenwell Green
London EC1R 0HT

The right of John Ladd
to be identified as author of this work has been
asserted by him in accordance with the Copyright,
Designs and Patents Act 1988.

Typeset by
Derek Doyle & Associates, Liverpool.
Printed and bound in Great Britain by
Antony Rowe Limited, Wiltshire

The Forty Riders

To everyone in the remote town of Powder Springs he was, and always had been, Joe Smith, husband, father and baker. Not even his wife and sons knew his true identity and his secret would have remained with him to his grave but for one sunny morning, when Trent Hardin led forty riders into town to execute the most daring and ambitious robbery of his career. Backed by an army of deadly outlaws he planned to take control of the town and its citizens and was determined that nothing, and no one, would stand in his way.

As darkness fell, and terror enveloped Powder Springs, none of the outlaws could suspect that one man was preparing to finish a job he had started many years earlier. Soon they would face the once infamous man, and only then would they all know who Joe Smith really was and what a deadly enemy he would prove to be.

Dedicated to:

Wild Bill Black

ONE

The community of Powder Springs had existed for nearly thirteen years. It had always been a small town surviving on the very edge of humanity. Always a quiet haven compared to most Texas towns, Powder Springs had remained untouched until an Eastern railroad company drove a track past the score of wooden buildings. Even calculating the few farms dotted around the town itself, its population had never managed to reach more than 300 at its peak and was usually only half that number.

The first settlers had discovered this place, with its natural spring amid the only fertile soil for a hundred miles around, by accident. They stayed, knowing it was doubtful there was anything better however far west they might travel.

Powder Springs became a reality within weeks of the small wagon-train arriving in the fertile valley. Isolated from the outside world for the first five years of its existence the town became totally self-sufficient, needing nothing the rest of the world had to offer.

There was a tranquillity within the valley which bonded every one of its citizens together more strongly than any glue known to man. Each man, woman and child knew all there was to know about others, or at least they thought they did. In even the most serene of communities there is always something or someone who has a secret which is beyond the wildest imaginations of others.

Powder Springs was no exception to this rule. The quiet town offered more than just a peaceful life to the settlers who had built their own paradise within its fertile boundaries but also a place where those trying to escape their past could blend in unnoticed.

So it was for one lost soul.

Then the relative peace that Powder Springs had enjoyed for half a decade evaporated as the railroad company discovered the flat valley and ran their iron tracks straight through. There was a reason for the new route which none of the citizens of the small town had any idea about.

Soon the trains would pass through Powder Springs without slowing their progress. Never stopping. After a while it was as if they just became part of the scenery as they steamed through the town along their gleaming rails. Before long, even the curiosity waned.

But ignorance was no protection.

They totalled forty in number as they thundered over the dry mesa road on their way to the small town of Powder Springs. Every one of the riders had been hand-picked by the horseman in the front of the pack, who was dressed entirely in black leather. His name was reputed to be Trent Hardin, although men in his profession tended to change their names more often than their clothes.

Whatever his true identity, he was undoubtedly the leader of this band of riders. None of the others came close to him even when beckoned. He had earned his reputation the hard way and the ten notches carved into the grip of his solitary pistol was more than ample proof of it.

Yet there was more to the complex character of Trent Hardin than met the eye. He was no mere outlaw but a man of undoubted intelligence who had chosen this direction for his life when anything had been possible.

Hardin was here in this alien landscape for one purpose only and he alone knew exactly what that was. A plan had been brewing like a good beer in his mind for months and with his usual expertise he had managed to hone it to perfection.

He knew that to let his followers in on its details too soon could prove fatal, to himself.

These were his men but he did not trust any of them. He had seen how deadly any of these individuals could be.

The hard core of his usual gang consisted of five men, each of them ruthless and totally loyal to him.

Ben Franks, Cole Dewer, Floyd Singleton, Gates Brown and Spangler Brough all stayed close to the rider who led them with such fervour. The other riders were all known to Hardin and had all worked for him in the past on various capers but this was the first and possibly the last time they would all be brought together, lured to his service by the promise of an equal split.

The trailing outlaws knew that Hardin was a genius at planning and executing robberies of incredible daring. They had seldom gone wrong and most men who rode with him survived to spend their ill-gotten gains. Yet for all their confidence in Hardin, none could imagine why he had brought so many of them together for this particular job.

They had been plucked from a dozen towns across Texas for this mission by Hardin. Their assembling had taken over a month to organize and the journey which was now coming to an end had seen ten days of hard riding.

The prairie had given way to a more fertile land as the forty ruthless killers drove their mounts onward. Powder Springs was a strange destination for so many evil souls yet Hardin had his reasons for going to this remote town.

Hardin dragged his reins up to his chin and halted his dark-grey mare. His men all stopped their mounts a few feet behind his rising dust.

Hardin stared down from the crest of a small green hill and watched the morning sun begin to trace across the still-sleeping town of Powder Springs. Smoke still rose from several solid stone chimney-stacks as the forty riders eyed the small peaceful town.

Hardin pulled out a slim cigar and bit off its tip before placing it between his teeth. He struck a match and drew in the smoke whilst he concentrated on the sleeping town below them.

'Is this it?' Floyd Singleton asked as he watched Hardin enjoying his smoke.

'Shut the hell up, Floyd,' Gates Brown snapped. He steered his horse between Hardin and the grouchy rider.

Hardin used his cigar to point at the twenty or more buildings.

'That's Powder Springs.'

None of the riders said a word.

'Notice the one thing which makes the town interesting?' Hardin asked.

Again, none of them replied.

Hardin pointed his cigar at the rail track which snaked its way through the heart of the town.

'See that track?'

There was a muttering through the ranks of the riders which verged on agreement to the simple statement.

'So?' Spangler Brough spat.

Hardin turned to the rider with dark hair and dismissed the hostility. They were all sore and tired after such a long arduous trek.

'That just happens to be the main Southern Pacific line down to the new mint outside Austin, boys,' Hardin informed his men. 'One track in and out of the mint.'

Suddenly the riders realized why Hardin was grinning so widely as he sat astride his mount. This was a far bigger job than any of them had imagined.

'Does the train stop here?' Cole Dewer asked.

'Nope,' said Hardin through the smoke which trailed from his lips. 'I figure it never has stopped in Powder Springs.'

'I don't get it,' Brough admitted.

Hardin straightened up in his saddle. 'Usually the train passes straight through because it's laden down with carriage after carriage of fresh-minted money, boys. I reckon the last thing they'd want to do is stop. They never have.'

'What good is that to us?' Gates mumbled.

'None at all, that's why we are going to make it stop.' Hardin tossed away his cigar and dug his spurs into the flanks of his mare and led the riders down towards the town.

TWO

Not everyone in Powder Springs was asleep. One man in his late thirties happened to be wide awake as usual as he finished his night's work in his small neat bakery behind his equally tidy café. For the ten years since he had arrived in this quiet part of the Lone Star State he had worked throughout the night baking bread and pastries for the citizens of the small town.

Upstairs in the two-bedroom apartment his wife and two young sons slept peacefully, unaware of what was heading towards their little town. Olive had been in Powder Springs from its very birth and met her husband within hours of his arrival. Their two small sons Adam and Alex had arrived over the following two years. Yet although they were the people closest to the quiet baker, even they had no idea of the secret he kept locked up in the darkest corners of his soul.

He had been known as Joe Smith for the ten

years he had lived within the small community and there were days when he almost believed this was actually his given name. The illusion never lasted long though.

Even after a decade, Smith had found it was impossible to lie to himself as he had done so masterfully to everyone else. There was a place in his mind where his true identity still existed and refused to die.

To everyone in Powder Springs he was the baker named Joe Smith and that was the way he preferred it to remain.

It had taken ten years of hard work to become the trusted man with flour on his face who made the best bread anyone had ever tasted, but he knew the truth.

A truth which he had long thought would go to the grave with him. Until this fateful morning, there might just have been a slim chance that that desire would be honoured. The problem was, the forty riders who were approaching the small town would soon force this quiet man to act.

As Joe Smith moved through the café and pulled up the blinds to allow the morning sun in, he felt a strange unease coming over him. He had felt the clutching in his guts many times over the years. A fear that the people who had grown to respect him might discover who and what he had actually been before riding into their midst.

14

What would their reaction be if they found out that the quiet unassuming baker had lied to them?

Even worse, what would Olive think of the man she had wed if she knew that everything he had told her about his life had been an invention?

Joe Smith felt a cold chill ripple up his spine.

Unlocking the door, Joe Smith stepped out on to the boardwalk and stared up and down the winding street as he had done a thousand times before. Beyond the buildings opposite he knew the iron rail-track lay waiting for the next train to pass. When the trains ran through Powder Springs every wooden structure shook. To Joe Smith it had grown to be a constant reminder that even here, the outside world existed. That one day the trains might decide to stop and allow people from his old life to find him.

It was a reminder that chilled him to the bone.

How long might it be before someone arrived and recognized him? Expose him? As long as those trains did not stop in Powder Springs there was still hope that his secret would remain just that; his secret.

Soon the customers would begin to filter into his café and start to buy his bread and drink his coffee. After an hour or so his wife would come down from upstairs with their sons and take over the daily ritual and allow him to go and get some sleep.

That was the way it had always happened.

Today would be different.

His mind drifted back to the day he had ridden into the town. It had been the last day of the existence he had endured for so many years. Joe Smith shuddered and swallowed hard. For ten years he had tried vainly to block out all memories of his previous life but still the images came back to haunt him. He leaned on the wall of the café which had become the centre of his world and sighed heavily.

Would he ever be able to forget those days? Days when just staying alive was a monumental achievement.

Was there nothing he could do to wipe them from his mind?

Joe Smith sighed heavily again as he walked back into the café and inhaled the aroma of his handiwork. Freshly baked bread and the serving of fragrant hot coffee had fed and clothed his small family. They had little but what they had was honestly earned.

Then, for some reason he could not fathom, he felt drawn back into his bakery. Smith stared down at the flour-covered wooden-board floor he himself had laid all those years ago. He knelt down in a corner, pulled a barrel to one side and brushed at the spilled flour with his hands.

For a moment his eyes stared down at the hand-crafted planks. Then, using his fingernails, he pulled two of them up and looked down at the leather saddle-bags which were still where he had placed them all those years earlier.

He unbuckled their flaps and reluctantly pulled out a set of dark clothes. He doubted if they would still fit him and he pushed them back into their hiding-place. Then he undid the other buckle, lifted the leather flap of the saddle-bag and looked down with a mixture of horror and pleasure. He could not resist pulling the hand-tooled leather gun-belt up and regarding the pair of pearl-handled pistols in their holsters.

For ten years they had remained within the bags, hidden from prying eyes. He remembered how, when he had first set eyes upon the town of Powder Springs, he had taken off his gun-belt and placed it in his saddle-bags.

The guns had remained there undisturbed until this moment. He pulled one of the still gleaming weapons free of its restraints and twirled it on his finger before sliding it back into its holster again.

It felt good.

So good he began to shake as his mind raced. Why had he suddenly been drawn to these weapons after so many years? They had served him well when he had worn them but that was in his old life, not his new one. Sweat began to trace down his face and his mouth went dry.

His days of wearing and using these guns were

far behind him, he thought. Smith considered what he now had, a loving wife and two handsome sons. These were blessings he cherished far beyond the fame his skill with these pistols had earned him.

Joe Smith, the quiet baker, never even owned a gun. He had never even had to raise his fists in anger since finding this tiny piece of paradise. Yet there was still a part of the man who missed the renown he had once enjoyed. A fame he had buried with his real name in order to find peace.

Suddenly, Joe Smith heard movement above him in the children's bedroom. Quickly he pushed the gun-belt back into the saddle-bag and replaced the floorboards. Then he rose to his full height and rolled the flour-barrel back.

He walked back into the café and poured himself a cup of black coffee. He raised it to his lips.

Through the aromatic steam he spied the first smiling face entering his humble café. He returned the warm smile.

'Morning, Joe,' the old lady said when she approached the long counter carrying her basket over her arm.

'Howdy, Martha.'

'Looks like it's going to be a fine day.' Martha Vine, the doctor's wife, smiled.

'Sure does. Sure does.'

For the briefest of moments the baker assumed this day was going to be just another ordinary day like all the thousands which had preceded it.

It was the first mistake the man who called himself Joe Smith had made in ten years.

THREE

An eerie silence swept through Powder Springs as the forty riders reined in their lathered up mounts on the outskirts of the town and surveyed it carefully. These were men who, between them, had entered scores of similar looking small towns over the years, yet never for the purpose which had brought them here. They had never taken an entire town hostage and as they sat brooding over the prospect, Trent Hardin pulled out the remnants of a half-bottle of whiskey from the pocket of his long coat and pulled its cork with his teeth.

As he spat the cork away and raised his bottle to his lips the men watched. It took only two large swallows to empty the liquor into his dry throat.

'I sure hope they got some booze in this place,' Hardin snarled as he tossed the bottle away.

'You better go easy on the rotgut, Trent,' Ben Franks advised knowingly.

'Maybe you're right.' Hardin nodded at the

21

rider closest to him as his eyes studied the figures rushing away from the very sight of them. 'Looks like they've spotted us.'

'This is too big a job for us to get drunk on.' Franks rubbed his dust caked face as he watched Hardin lighting a fresh cigar while his eyes fixed on Powder Springs.

It was as if the air itself was charged with an electricity which muted everyone who caught sight of the line of merciless horsemen. Even the birds in the trees appeared to stop singing as the line of heavily armed riders sat watching the wooden buildings of the town.

Although still early, there had been many of the town's citizens on the streets of Powder Springs going about their business as usual until their innocent eyes had spotted the unwelcome group of trail weary men.

Trent Hardin leaned across in his saddle to Ben Franks and exhaled a long line of cigar smoke as he began talking again.

'Quiet enough for you, Ben?'

'Sure is.'

'I bet there ain't no more than a handful of shotguns in this entire town,' Hardin sighed.

Franks nodded. 'You been here before?'

'Yep. I rode through here six months back when I was putting this whole deal together.' Hardin smiled. 'Nobody even saw me because it was in the dead of night.'

The riders began to understand the uniqueness of this place as they saw the morning sun glinting off the iron rail-tracks which passed through the town.

'This is a train robbery, huh?' Spangler Brough asked as he gripped his reins in his strong hands.

'In a way, it is. But there's a tad more to it than just sticking up a train,' Hardin explained.

'How many folks in this town?' Floyd Singleton piped up as he struck a match across his saddle horn and raised its flame to the cigarette between his lips.

'Maybe a hundred or so, I guess,' Hardin replied.

'So that's why you needed all of us?' Dewer nodded.

'How come you didn't just use half a dozen men to hold up the train? That's the way we always do it.' Gates Brown sniffed as he watched the few people who had been walking the streets when they had arrived fleeing into their homes.

'This ain't no ordinary train, Brown,' Hardin said as he sucked more smoke into his lungs. 'This is the bullion train to and from the mint. It's got guards on it.'

'How many guards?' Brough queried.

'As far as I was able to find out when I was in Austin, about twenty.' Hardin blew out smoke through his teeth. 'Heavily armed and mean. But I doubt if there's a brain amongst the lot of them though.'

The majority of the riders began to grasp the sheer magnitude of the job in hand while they watched their leader flicking ash from his cigar as he stared at the town like an eagle watching its chosen prey. To a man they knew even though he had outlined his plan to them, Hardin had not told them any of the details which meant the difference between success and failure to a group such as theirs.

They were indeed forty well armed experienced outlaws but without someone of Hardin's intelligence in control, they were simply forty targets. He alone knew how to make this work and he alone remained their leader.

'What's this town got to do with robbing a train?' Singleton asked innocently.

'You'll find out. You'll find out,' Hardin answered as he tapped his spurs into his grey mare and allowed the animal to begin the slow walk into Powder Springs. There were no more questions from the riders who followed Hardin.

The sight of so many riders entering their town caused the few who witnessed it to rush and inform the rest of Powder Springs' population. The news rushed like wildfire through the town. By the time the forty grim-faced riders had reached the centre of the town, nearly every living soul was standing on the boardwalks watching in silent awe. Every eye was on the forty riders, who

seemed to have at least two handguns apiece and
carbine rifles tucked in under their saddles. None
of the onlookers had ever seen such a well-armed
group of riders before.

With the exception of one curious observer. Joe
Smith was no stranger to men such as these.

Hardin led his men like a military commander
until he reached the very heart of the community.
Then he stopped his mount and began to stare
into the eyes of all who dared cast their attention
upon him. His were cold eyes, devoid of any emo-
tion as they swept over each face in turn.

His men gathered around him in a huge circle
and watched all sides for any trouble.

There was none.

Even before the riders had reached the middle
of Powder Springs, the man who was known as
Joe Smith had been standing on the boardwalk
outside his small café and bakery watching them
pass by.

Of all the citizens in this little town, he alone
knew what these men were. They were the sort of
men he had faced so many times when he himself
had been a feared gunfighter. He recognized their
sort easily.

They were scum, intent on doing as they
pleased, and he knew it.

Such men always brought death with them,
Smith thought. His only worry was why there
were so many. Even the James gang limited their

numbers to fewer than a dozen, even on the biggest of their jobs.

Smith strolled down the wooden walkways as the riders made their way through the quiet street. He kept pace with their sweating horses and studied each men with an eye used to seeing such vermin in his earlier days. He knew they were here for no good.

Nobody came to this remote place out of choice, he concluded as he walked past the fronts of buildings, weaving his way between people who were struck dumb at the very sight of so many well armed killers.

Joe Smith could not put names to any of the riders but he thought he recognized the man who led them. Desperately he tried to recall who the cigar-smoking rider was.

Smith was unafraid as he studied them. Their sort had never made him back away in the past, and now as he walked, covered in flour, he knew he had grown no less brave.

He stopped behind a group of women, and stared over their bonnets as Trent Hardin reined his grey mare to a halt in front of the white-washed schoolhouse.

As Hardin cast his calculating eyes over the residents of the town he had no idea someone from his past was standing covered in flour looking up at him. For the briefest of moments their eyes met as the rider glanced around and the confused expressions gazed back at his followers. Hardin had not given the baker more than a second of his attention but Smith had continued to look up at him with increasing curiosity.

He knew this face, Smith thought.

It had grown older, like his own, but it was still recognizable. Suddenly Joe Smith knew he was looking at the notorious Trent Hardin. Hardin was the man who had planned so many bank and train robberies for outlaw gangs ranging from the James brothers to the Hole in the Wall gang. The baker began to understand that the man was now creating his own meticulously planned jobs for himself.

Yet why did he require so many riders to back him up?

Smith moved away from the front of the porch overhang and allowed the morning shadows to shade his face from a man who just might remember who he had once been. It was doubtful that he would recall the wrinkled flour-covered face but Smith knew how smart Hardin was.

If anyone would see through the ravages of time, it was he.

Hardin removed his Stetson and cleared his throat.

'Good morning, friends,' he began. 'My name is of no concern to any of you folks. These are my men, each one deadlier than the next. We're here for a mighty good reason, but that ain't none of

your business either. What you have to understand is that if any of you try to interface with us,
you'll die. So if you want to go on living you better
take heed and do what we tell you. Remember,
friends, there ain't no other way. You do as we tell
you or you'll die.'

A muttering swept among the terrified onlookers as the men, women and children all began to
absorb Hardin's stark warning.

Joe Smith felt his mouth drying as he watched
the forty riders drawing their carbines from
beneath their saddles and holding them across
their bellies.

They were not bluffing, Smith thought to himself as his knowing eyes darted from one rider's
face to another. Every man who held his carbine
was ready to use it at the slightest provocation.

From across the street Smith heard the familiar voice of his wife's father, Lucas Green, bellow-
ing at the intruders. For the first time since setting eyes on Hardin and his entourage Smith felt
his blood run cold in his veins as the angry words
echoed around the wooden buildings. Then Joe
Smith caught sight of the old man with snow-
white hair marching towards the riders. He knew
there were too many people and horses between
himself and the old man to stop him venting his
wrath.

'Who do you think you are coming into our town
and threatening us, mister?' Lucas yelled in his

best preacher tones. A voice he used to great effect every Sunday when he conducted the simple church service in the small school. 'You cannot come here and order us around. Be gone.'

Smith watched the old man's arm rise and point in the direction the riders had just come from. Then he heard a sound which had not met his ears for over a decade. It was the sound of a carbine being cranked for action.

Trent Hardin had not uttered a word as he watched the face of the irate figure who was approaching him. He levelled his rifle to chest height and fired. Not once nor twice but repeatedly until the air was black with gunsmoke.

Each bullet tore through the old man. Even before the sixth had found its mark, it was obvious to the horrified audience that Lucas Green was dead. As his blood-soaked body hit the ground each of the riders cocked their carbines in unison, as if warning the rest of the town to do nothing.

Hardin rested the wooden rifle-stock on his thigh and then raised his voice above the sound of the noise of women crying all around them.

'That's what you will all get if there is any further defiance, my friends.'

Joe Smith moved through the people and then paused as his eyes took in the full horror of Hardin's ultimatum. The man he had known for ten years lay ripped apart by rifle bullets, lifeless and twisted in the centre of the street.

Smith walked as if in a trance to the body of the man who had become like a father to him since he had married the man's only child, Olive. As he knelt down next to the old man's body he heard the sound of hoof-beats coming up behind him.

'What do you think you're doing?' Hardin's voice asked from atop the dark-grey mare.

Joe Smith scooped up the limp body in his arms and then stood and faced the rider.

'Just taking my father home,' Smith responded bluntly.

'You intending on causing trouble like your pa?' Hardin growled down at the top of the baker's head.

'Nope. I'm just a baker. What could I do?' Smith replied as he cradled the body in his strong arms as its blood soaked into his apron.

Hardin laughed. 'Take the old fool away, baker.'

The man who was known as Joe Smith turned and walked slowly down the street with what remained of a once good man in his arms. As he got within a few feet of the front of his café he heard the laughter of forty riders behind him and then saw the face of his wife in the doorway.

FOUR

It did not take the forty intruders very long to overwhelm any opposition the people of Powder Springs might have mustered. Within an hour of their arrival the outlaws had searched nearly every building and confiscated the town's few weapons.

Hardin had calculated perfectly how many men he required to subdue the town. As the clocks struck nine that same morning he was in total control.

Most of the stunned townspeople had been herded into the schoolhouse to be searched before being allowed back on to the streets. Hardin knew this sort of people, he had encountered their like a dozen or more times over the years. They worked hard and were easily stripped of their savings. They might raise their voices but most had never held any sort of firearm before, let alone used one. The West was littered with their kind and Powder Springs was no exception.

'Anybody checked the bakery?' Hardin asked Cole Dewer as he leaned on the white picket-fence that surrounded the schoolhouse.

'You serious?' Dewer asked as he watched the man clad in black leather staring down the quiet street towards Joe Smith's café.

'Sure am. Take a couple of boys and search the building from top to bottom,' Hardin said as he placed a cigar between his teeth. 'I don't trust that tall baker.'

'He's just another dumb tenderfoot like all these folks.'

Hardin stared straight into Dewer's eyes.

'Do as I tell you.'

Dewer shrugged and whistled at a couple of their men to follow him as he began walking down towards the sun-bleached store-sign which read CAFÉ AND BAKERY above the porch overhang.

Joe Smith held his wife close as he watched the outlaws heading from across the street towards the café. For a moment his eyes flashed into the bakery and the corner where the flour barrel still concealed his secret; the clothes and weaponry which had once been his trademark.

Would these men discover the guns?

If so, what would they do not only to himself but his small family?

The thought chilled the tall baker. He knew

32

men like Trent Hardin never allowed anyone to show their defiance without putting bullets into them. He was the most dangerous type of outlaw, he had brains. Hardin knew the best way to keep on top of everyone was to dish out instant punishment. Even the riders who blindly followed him were not exempt from the instant death sentence his fast hands could unleash.

What had happened to Lucas Green had been at least fast enough to have offered little pain to the old man. Smith knew if they discovered his hidden guns beneath the bakery floor, his own death would come slowly and painfully. It was the perfect way to teach total obedience to all the onlookers. Men like Hardin knew a hundred ways to prolong an execution.

As the three heavily armed men pushed their way into the café and ignored the lifeless body which lay beneath a sheet upon the bread counter, they forced their way through the building looking for weapons of any description. They still laughed at the sight of the man who was the town's baker, but their laughter did not effect Smith.

He was beginning to hatch a plan of his own in his tired mind as they searched. It seemed outrageous to even dare consider standing up against such numbers but Smith had always enjoyed risking his neck in the past. Smith had taught himself to become a baker, but that was not where his natural ability lay. For the first time in ten years he felt that proficiency, so long denied, swelling up within him again.

'You got any guns in this place, baker?' Cole Dewer grinned at the face of the tall quiet man.

'What would a baker want guns for?' Smith replied in a low calm voice as he felt his wife trembling beside him.

'There's a lot of pretty females in this town, baker,' another of the outlaws noted aloud. 'I kind of like your woman.'

Smith gritted his teeth and narrowed his eyes as Dewer pushed the outlaw away.

'Get on with searching, boy,' Dewer ordered as he too gave the attractive female a second look before leading his confederates up the stairs to the living accommodation.

'Why did they kill my pa, Joe?' Olive began to sob again as she buried her face into his broad chest.

'Because he had the guts to stand up to them, honey,' Smith replied quietly.

'Promise me you will not do anything, Joe,' she begged.

'What could I do?' His words comforted her shaking body as he listened to the sound of boots moving around their rooms above the small café.

Joe Smith stood with an arm around his beautiful wife as his two young sons hid in terror behind him. He said nothing as he watched the outlaws returning from the rooms above before entering his bakery. As they moved around the tables and large ovens, he just observed them silently. This was not the time to open his mouth, he thought.

These were not ordinary men but savage killing thieves who had little or no respect for anything or anyone.

As they moved around the large barrel, Smith felt his heart beginning to race. They saw nothing out of the ordinary and walked back into the café.

'Coffee smells good,' Dewer remarked as his two cohorts continued back into the street.

'Help yourself.' Smith nodded as the gunman poured himself a cup and swirled it down his throat quickly as if immune to its heat.

'Pretty good coffee, baker,' Dewer said as he picked up a loaf of bread and carried it out into the street. The blood on its crust did not seem to worry him at all.

'Who are they, Joe?' Olive asked as her hands searched and found the two small children who cowered behind their father's legs. 'Who are these people?'

'Vermin, Olive. Just vermin.' Joe Smith walked to the door and stared out at the deadly creatures who seemed to be everywhere, keeping the people of Powder Springs under control. 'You had better take the boys upstairs where it's safe.'

'Who are they? What do they want of us?' she

asked again. Her eyes stared at the blood-soaked sheet which covered the remains of her beloved father.

'I recognize the leader. His name is Trent Hardin,' Smith said in a low, shaking voice. A voice which reflected his anger. 'He's a planner of bank hold-ups and the like. He must have branched out on his own by the looks of it.'

'How could you know him?' Olive asked as she stared into the face of her man. 'How on earth could you know that, Joe?'

Joe Smith did not reply. He squeezed her shoulder but did not answer her question.

For the first time in all the years she had known the tall quiet man who she loved above all others, Olive began to wonder if there was more to his life than he had told her.

FIVE

The knuckles on Joe Smith's hands were white as he clenched his fists in anger and watched the body being hurriedly lowered into the shallow grave. There had not been time nor permission to bury Lucas Green properly. A handful of his friends had come to the café and helped him carry the blood-soaked remains to the small graveyard set in a leafy meadow a few hundred yards from the town. Hardin had sent five of his most ruthless men to ensure the body was buried without any problems.

Smith's eyes moved from one outlaw to the next as his friends gathered around, trying to console him. Yet he felt no sorrow as he shovelled the damp soil over the old man who was wrapped in a blanket.

Only anger.

There were many more townspeople than outlaws in Powder Springs but numbers meant nothing in this game. This was something far beyond the knowledge of ordinary people like his friends. This was something only men like Hardin understood because his sort thrived on the cultivation of fear.

They knew how to chill their enemy into dying long before their bullets tore them apart.

As Joe Smith patted the soil down on the makeshift grave he straightened up and stared at the men who clung on to their cocked rifles like females cradling their young.

He knew how to defeat their sort.

It had once been so easy to do so, it had become almost second nature. Now things were different; he was older, and had never faced such a huge show of strength. But he had something none of these animals had. Joe Smith had right on his side.

He and the handful of mourners walked back to the town, surrounded by the gunmen who trained their long rifles on them. He began to think clearly for the first time since setting eyes on Trent Hardin again after so many years.

There were too many of them to face square on. That would prove fatal and he knew it. He would have to strike quickly and then disappear just as fast.

Smith knew there was no way he could allow any of Hardin's men to see his face. The one thing he had to ensure was keeping his identity secret.

If even one of the riders were to recognize the quiet baker, it would just bring them all down on his family.

As he walked with the shovel over his shoulder with his friends around him, Smith knew he dare not put Olive or his sons at risk.

Whatever he did, he had to make sure nobody, not even his fellow townspeople, suspected who was behind the surprise attack on Hardin and his cronies.

Could he still handle his prized weapons? Or had he lost all his skill to the passage of time? He vowed that he would at least try to stop these killers with whatever ability he had left in his hands.

He had to try; there was nobody else.

Hardin stood beside the last wooden building as the southbound train steamed slowly through Powder Springs on its way to the new mint on the outskirts of Austin. The huge engine with its brightly painted cattle-guard hissed as it passed the ruthless outlaw. The engineer stared down at the man dressed in leather as he pulled on the whistle cord and sent the distinctive sound bouncing off the buildings.

Hardin touched the brim of his Stetson to the engineer as Ben Franks walked up beside him.

'What's the time?' asked Hardin.

'Nearly noon,' Franks replied, checking the face

of his pocket watch. He snapped shut the silver cover.

Hardin nodded as he raised a cigar to his lips and sucked in on the strong smoke.

'We've got roughly fifteen hours before the train returns along these tracks, Ben.'

'Due back through here at three in the morning?' asked Franks.

'Yep. But it'll be full to overflowing with fresh-minted money when it returns. Who knows how much money?' Hardin laughed and smoke trailed from his mouth. 'I got me a feeling we'll all be mighty rich bastards this time tomorrow, Ben.'

Franks looked concerned. 'That's a long time to keep these folks tame, Trent. I still ain't sure why you wanted to take the whole damn town prisoner like this.'

'Because it's part of my plan,' Hardin grated.

'I reckon you ain't about to tell me the details, huh?' Ben Franks shuffled his boots as he looked from beneath his hat-brim at the smiling outlaw.

'You reckon right,' Hardin said stiffly. He watched the train disappearing into the distance.

'I'm just a tad concerned about hanging around here for so long,' Franks admitted. He fumbled with the silver watch-chain as he tucked it into his vest pocket.

Hardin turned and stared at the men he had scattered around the town. Men who all clung to their rifles waiting if not praying for someone to

40

do something they could punish with a volley of lethal lead.

'You worried about our boys, Ben?'

'Sure. Some of the men Spangler roped in on this job are real edgy critters, Trent.' Franks sighed anxiously as he walked beside the athletic Hardin. 'I got me a feeling we'll have trouble with some of them for sure.'

Hardin nodded as smoke trailed from his teeth.

'Yeah, I know what you mean. I've ridden with all of them over the years and they ain't the best of the bunch. But if they start anything with me, I'll finish it.'

'Spangler ain't exactly a top hand either. I never have trusted him.' Franks sighed heavily.

'Let me worry about Spangler and his choice of gunhands. I figure we might just require a few of them to give those bullion guards something to aim at when the train comes back.' Hardin was grinning from ear to ear as he spoke these words.

'You'd sacrifice Spangler and his boys?' Franks raised an eyebrow.

'Why not? Ain't none of them worth a plug nickel.'

The two men headed along the boardwalk and paused outside the locked doors of the tiny saloon. Hardin stared at the door and then drew one of his pistols from its holster and aimed at the brass keyhole. Squeezing his trigger silently, Hardin watched as the doors began to open and the lock fell in fragments at their feet.

'What you doing?' Franks asked as Hardin strolled through the gunsmoke into the saloon.

'The boys have been riding hard for weeks, Ben. They deserve a drink or two,' Hardin replied.

Franks walked to Hardin's side and looked at his emotionless face as it studied the wall filled with bottles.

'This ain't the sort of job to get liquored up on.'

'You said that already.' Hardin pulled the cigar from his mouth and blew the grey smoke at the floor before turning to face the older man. 'I make the decisions. Just remember that, Ben. I figure you'll live a lot longer.'

SIX

By four in the afternoon most of Hardin's men had washed their thirst away in the saloon, while the citizens of Powder Springs tried to go about their business. All forty of their horses had been watered and fed; now they filled the usually empty fenced-off pasture behind the livery stable. Hardin had placed two guards in the stable building to ensure nobody took one of their horses in a futile attempt to raise the alarm and get help.

The leader of the huge army of outlaws himself somehow managed to avoid drinking. He sat in a hard chair on the boardwalk outside the building. He was wise enough to know that he could get far more out of these hired killers if they were drunk than if they were sober.

It was a gamble which few men in his position would have dared to take, but Hardin was unlike others of his kind. He liked taking risks.

That was why he had continued to stage hold-ups long after he had become wealthy enough to retire to an easier life. These men were scum and he was the first to admit it, but they could all handle themselves.

Franks was the only man who had remained with him for every one of the carefully planned jobs they had executed, yet Hardin only just tolerated him.

Hardin had always felt he was superior to everyone else. He felt that he alone had the right to make life-or-death decisions because he truly believed he was cleverer than any other living being. So far, nobody had dared challenge him.

'We got ourselves a lot of liquored-up men, Trent,' Franks said. He stared into the saloon where most of their gang continued drinking.

'Good. I want them drunk.' Hardin gave a sigh and looked up at Trent. 'Drunk men ain't as afraid when the lead starts flying, Ben.'

'But drunk men are a lot harder to control.'

'Maybe.'

'We could lose most of them in the shoot-out with them train guards,' Ben Franks said anxiously.

Hardin stood and placed a hand upon his gun grip. 'I figure we could lose maybe thirty or more men on this job, Ben.'

'That many?'

'I sure hope so.' Hardin grinned again. He looked up and down the street and at the terrified creatures who moved along its wooden board-walks. 'We are going to have us a battle when the train comes back. I got me a lot of cannon-fodder which I'm willing to sacrifice for the greater good. The greater good being whatever it takes to see me alive and rich when the dust settles.'

Franks removed his hat and scratched his thinning hair.

'I don't get it. You want our own men to get themselves up and killed? Why?'

There was a long silence as Trent Hardin stared up at the sun just above the schoolhouse spire. It would be dark in less than two hours, he figured. It would still be dark when the train made its way back through the small town as it headed north.

'We've been together for a long time, Ben,' Hardin said, and his face suddenly went serious. 'I ain't never headed you into a suicidal job, have I?'

'That's true,' Franks admitted.

'Trust me on this one, will you?'

Ben Franks bit his lower lip.

'You ain't answered my question, Trent. Why are you willing to see our own men get killed?'

'Out of the thirty-eight riders we brought here, I reckon I can trust maybe less than half a dozen. This job is big and it requires a small army to make it work, but once my plan is set in motion we can afford to lose the less reliable critters we brought along.' Hardin turned his gaze to the café again and wondered why the baker covered in flour still intrigued him.

'Does that mean if they don't get themselves killed you'll still give them all an equal share?' Franks began to understand his companion slightly better.

'Sure. Equal shares for all the survivors, Ben.' Hardin nodded vigorously.

'Good.'

'But on the other hand ...' Hardin smiled as he thought about the forty mounts they had ridden into this town.

Ben Franks tilted his head back and looked at Hardin.

'Other hand?'

'Yeah. On the other hand, just think of how much more money all those horses can carry if they ain't got riders in their saddles, Ben.' Hardin began to chuckle as he returned the gaze of his most loyal follower.

'Yeah,' drawled Franks.

SEVEN

'There's something you're not telling me, Joe,' Olive Smith said as she fixed her family its early evening meal. 'I think it must be very important.'

There had always been a fine line between lying to a loved one and avoiding telling them a truth which might cause them either stress or actual harm. Joe Smith had walked this tightrope for ten years now and it grew no easier. Yet there were things about his former life which could do nothing but cause his wife increased fear. She had suffered enough this day, he thought.

'What do you mean, honey?' Smith asked trying to at least look as if she were imagining things by his expression. For the first time since the day they met, she saw through the façade.

'I might not have had much of an education, Joe, but I'm not stupid.' Olive frowned as she began placing the slices of well browned ham on to plates from the griddle. 'You knew the gang's

47

leader by name. You also knew what he did.'

Smith because uneasy. 'So?'

'How did you know these things?' she pressed, setting the plates on the kitchen table. 'In all the years I've known you I have never seen you read a newspaper or anything else for that matter.'

He said nothing as he watched their sons beginning their long-overdue meal. Both the boys looked like her, he thought. Same colour hair. Same small noses. Same magical blue eyes. He thought: how fragile the people he loved were.

'Today has been horrific, honey. You need to relax,' Smith said softly as he tried vainly to change the subject.

Olive returned the griddle to the stove top before moving closer to the man she was beginning to question after ten years of total harmony.

'You have not told me the truth about your life before coming to Powder Springs, have you?' The question was blunt yet accurate.

'Sometimes a man ain't proud of what he once was, Olive. Sometimes he has to create a better past for himself.'

She stared straight up at him. 'You lied to me, Joe. All these years you have been lying to me.'

'I guess I did but not for any bad reasons.' Smith placed his hands onto the small shoulders and looked down into the face which seemed even more beautiful now than when he had first encountered her.

'I trusted you. Now my father is dead and I find out that you know his killer. How do you know his killer, Joe?' Somehow Olive managed to control the torrent of emotions which were ripping her world apart.

'Do you trust me, Olive?' Smith asked gently.

The question was direct. She looked up into his familiar face; a face which, unlike her own, had grown visibly older as he had worked hard to provide for her and their children.

'You know I have always trusted you but this does not make any sense, Joe,' she replied. The face of the man she adored was troubled. She had never seen this look in his features before and it worried her. 'I want answers. I must know the truth you have hidden from me.'

'I know it does not add up.' Smith pulled her into his arms and wondered how he could have managed to keep the truth of his past from her for so long. 'I cannot explain now but I promise you that when I am able, I shall tell you everything.'

'Why not now, Joe?' Olive whispered.

'There are some things it's healthier not to know,' he said as their eyes met. 'These men kill in the same way most normal men breathe. Without a second thought. The truth could bring these killers down on you and the boys the same way they turned on your father. I recognized Hardin but, thankfully, he did not know who I am. Unlike him, I've kind of aged. That is my advantage.'

'I do not understand, my love. What do you need an advantage for, Joe?'

Smith shook his head. 'Can you trust me when I beg you not to ask me anything further? I promise you, if I thought there was no danger, I would explain everything right now. But there is danger, and you must remember only one thing, whatever happens. Your husband is nothing but a baker.'

'But that's exactly what you are, Joe. Just a baker.'

'That's right. That's all I am.' He kissed her hair and he felt his throat begin to dry. That was what he was now, but once he had been something else. Something which made men like those forty riders quake in their high-heeled boots.

As Olive rested her body against his she could feel his heart pounding. Slowly she placed her fingers inside his shirt and allowed her fingers to touch his skin. The beating heart quickened.

'I'm going down to the bakery after we eat,' Smith said, pulling up a chair. 'You must all stay up here and, whatever happens, do not venture down the stairs.'

Olive felt her own heart beginning to beat faster. 'If that's what you want, Joe.'

'That's what I want.'

The shadows grew longer and the sky began to turn a vivid red above the wisps of cloud. Night

50

was coming and yet the day seemed unwilling to admit defeat. Joe Smith had locked the door of his café and pulled down the blind over the display window. He stood by the locked door and looked out on to the troubled street.

The street lanterns were being lit as usual by Hoot Crawford, the livery stable man, but the flickering light did nothing to make things clearer out there in the growing unrest. As the old man lit the lanterns there was one thing in marked contrast to the usual Powder Springs evenings; this night Hoot Crawford had the company of a man carrying a Winchester trained on his bowed spine.

There was a noise in the street which Smith had not heard since arriving in this once peaceful place. The sound of drunken rowdy men intent on doing something he had yet to figure.

Why were they here in Powder Springs?

What would Hardin want to come here?

Each question Smith asked himself seemed to yield no answers because he was unaware of the precious cargo the northbound train carried as it steamed through his town every few days. If he had been privy to that knowledge it would have all fallen into place like a jigsaw puzzle.

Smith pulled the door-blind down, then paused a moment to watch the men in and around the saloon.

Trent Hardin sat beneath a lantern on the boardwalk outside the saloon whilst other men ran in and out of the drinking hole. As Smith watched the man dressed in leather, he felt sweat rolling down his spine. The sky was now purple as the sun drowned in the sea of darkness. It was not yet completely dark but getting there fast.

As Joe Smith secured the blind he carefully observed the street through a small gap in the shade beside the window. What he witnessed worried him greatly.

Hardin's men were drunk and beginning to run amok as their leader just sat and smoked his long cigar.

The tall baker felt his heart pounding inside his shirt beneath the long apron. He thought about his attractive wife upstairs with his sons. There were many other females as handsome as his wife in the town. He knew them all by name and he also knew what fate awaited them as darkness enveloped the small town.

Smith knew what came next to men who had drunk themselves into the sewer of depravity.

They would soon be seeking out these women and Hardin would not stop them. The outlaw leader might even join them in their quest to satisfy their carnal appetites. They had controlled the town since early morning and already killed his father-in-law. Now they had the cover of darkness to mask their actions and with the liquor swamping whatever morality remained within their darkened souls, they would act. Smith knew they would act soon. Perhaps they had already started.

He sighed heavily as he walked through the dark café into the bakery, where his bread-ovens still burned.

He had to do something now.

Fast.

There was no more time to think. No time to fret over what might happen to himself. For the first time in over ten years he felt the old excitement awakening within him. The man he had once been had found a reason to exist again. The abhorrence of his past was evaporating as he began to realize that only he could stop Hardin and his followers; only he had the expertise to face down these killers.

Smith stood beside the large ovens and felt their heat embrace him. He had not expanded around his waist, as had most men in the town over the years, because of his working over these hot ovens. Maybe his old clothing might still fit, he thought.

He stepped to the corner of the sweltering room, stooped and dragged the flour barrel away from the loose floorboards. For a second Smith hesitated as he looked down at the dark circle in the flour on the boards.

Then he lifted the loose boards again and pulled the saddle-bags out of the hole. He stood up and placed the bags on top of his large table.

He took the clothing from one of the bags and stared at the dark shirt and pants. They were exactly as he had left them all those years ago. He kicked off his flour-covered shoes and began to feel a long-forgotten excitement rising like sap within him. As he stripped off his baker's clothes he knew the old ones inside his saddle-bags would still fit.

As he dragged on the musty dark pants he felt the renewed energy filling his veins. Carefully he did up the brass studs over his firm abdomen. If anything, he had actually lost weight since he last wore these trousers, Smith concluded. He slipped on the cool shirt, buttoned it up and tucked its tail into his pants.

Smith then pulled his old cowboy-boots from a shelf and blew the dust from them. He had not worn these high-heeled creations for years, but tonight was different. The leather felt strange as he slid them on but at least he now seemed even taller. This was another thing which could disguise his identity from anyone who might decide to punish his loved ones.

He looked back into the first saddle-bag satchel and found the black bandanna he had once worn so religiously. He tied it loosely about his neck. This time he would wear it differently, though, he would wear it like a road-agent to cover his features.

He could not afford to overlook any minute

detail if his plan was going to work and not bring retribution down on the heads of his small family.

He unbuckled the small rusted catch on the second saddle-bag and, lifting it, Smith stared down at the shooting rig which had adorned his hips for so many fruitful years. It was a hand-tooled belt with two holsters and matching .45s. Beside the expensive guns and belt lay an almost full box of cartridges. When new this unique belt and guns had cost him plenty, but he had always made more than enough money back then from his gun skills.

The gunbelt he now held in his hands made a cold chill run up his spine. He strapped it on and tied the leather laces around his thighs. The guns were still loaded and the belt was filled with bullets, but Smith knew he required all the bullets in the cartridge box as well, if he were to stand any chance of stopping all these men.

He emptied the bullets from the cardboard box into his pants pockets. He prayed there would be time to reload his guns once the shooting started.

He moved quickly to the wooden shelving which held his many bread-trays and tins. His keen eyes stared at the cluttered shelving illuminated by the glowing ovens until he spotted what he was looking for. A tattered box on the middle shelf was carefully pulled down and opened to reveal the black small-brimmed 'John B' Stetson hat he had worn throughout his former life.

He placed it on his head and raised his bandanna over his mouth and nose. He knew there was nobody who would recognize him now. With the exception of one man.

Trent Hardin might recognize the apparel of someone he had encountered many years earlier; a gunfighter who was his equal with guns. But now the bandanna would conceal the face. A face which no longer resembled that of the man who had once filled a hundred evil souls with fear.

Fate had saved Hardin's bacon back then. He had been spared mainly due to the fact that he had planned his escape with such genius; not even the man who was now known as Smith could catch him.

No amount of planning could save him this time.

Now it was time for the man whom everyone regarded as merely a baker to see if he still had that old skill in his hands. As Smith stood in the dark bakery he flicked off the leather safety loops from his gun-hammers and held his hands above the guns like a vulture on a warm thermal breeze.

They hovered above the gun-grips for a few seconds before he allowed a former lifetime's practising to strike as quickly as a rattler.

He slapped leather and found the pistols in his hands. He had drawn both weapons and cocked the hammers with his thumbs in the blink of an eye. His index fingers had instinctively found both triggers and he knew he had lost none of his once-famed speed.

Smith sighed in relief as he carefully uncocked the gun hammers.

He twirled the deadly guns backwards and put them back into the holsters.

The old prowess remained true, he thought as he quietly opened the back door, stepped out into the darkness, then locked the door behind him. He placed the key inside his pants back pocket and looked around the area.

It was now completely dark.

The man who had become known as Joe Smith the baker began to move through the shadows like a panther stalking its prey.

He was ready.

EIGHT

Moving through the shadows, Smith felt as if he had stepped back in time to a place where he had once been the very best at what he did. To the masked man known as Joe Smith it seemed as if it were only yesterday that he had last worn the familiar clothing and lethal pair of matched .45s.

Chilling sounds drifted around Powder Springs and each one made Smith even more determined to get this daunting task over with as fast as humanly possible, before Hardin's men decided to visit his home and his distraught wife.

Every few yards he would crouch and hover with his right-hand cocked pistol in his firm grip. The sounds of various inebriated outlaws echoed off the wooden buildings all around him, making it difficult to work out exactly where they all were. Staring through a narrow gap between two houses, Smith spied the lantern-lit images of men moving around in pairs. He gritted his teeth and ran down the dark alley. He threw himself into the black shadows beside the water-trough.

He slid beneath a porch and crawled the length of the general store before scrambling out and heading in the direction of the schoolhouse. It seemed as if, every few paces, Smith was forced to take cover in the shadows before being able to continue. As he reached the corner of the schoolhouse he looked across into the street which was bathed in the gentle flickering light of the numerous lanterns. Each lantern posed a deadly danger to the lone man as he tried to move unnoticed about the town.

Powder Springs was crawling with Hardin's men as they trawled the streets looking for females to satisfy their liquor-soaked yearnings. The forty riders had seen the entire population gathered before them that very morning when they had arrived and immediately taken control. They knew that at the very least half the townspeople were females aged from five to seventy.

Joe Smith knew from experience that their sort could not resist such temptation. These were depraved drifters who had long forgotten what it meant to be civilized. Now they took what they wanted whenever the opportunity presented itself.

It was this knowledge which drove the man in the mask on. He alone could stop them. He alone was brave or bold enough even to try.

From this vantage-point, Smith could hear the sound of a couple of outlaws real close, noisily hunting down females of any age and of any appearance within the town's boundaries. Every so often he heard muffled cries from females who had obviously been cornered by Hardin's men.

Yet no matter how hard he tried Smith's eyes could not locate what his ears told him was near. They seemed to be hunting in pairs and most had drunk enough liquor to make them less aware of his presence. Smith knew he was too late to help the females whose cries hung on the night air, but he would try to stop any further violations if possible.

Angrily, Smith gripped one of his trusty guns as he ran round the rear of the school building until he had reached the opposite corner, bathed in darkness.

With every step, the masked figure could hear men's voices growing louder somewhere nearby. For a moment he was confused as the voices bounced off the walls, then he began to work out where they might be. Running along the side of the building, using the bushes and trees as cover until he was near the front of the building, he suddenly became aware of where his prey were.

It was only then that he espied the sight which had eluded him a few seconds earlier.

Two of the outlaws were sharing a bottle of whiskey as they made their way towards the home of his friend Ben Culver the owner of the general store. Culver was a man who had been in poor health for the past few years and was not the sort to be able to defend either his family or his property.

Smith felt his blood running cold in his veins as he realized where the two staggering men were heading.

Culver's house was set a few yards beyond the school and sported an apple tree in its fenced front-garden, amid a multitude of flowers. It was a terrifying thought that carved its way through Smith's mind as he stared across through the flickering light and black shadows.

Culver had little of any value, but he did have a wife and two pretty daughters in their late teens.

Like a pair of hounds seeking bitches in heat, the outlaws were drawn to the attractive house. They kicked the gate off its hinges and were now studying the house carefully, standing a few yards from its front door.

Joe Smith wondered if it might be coincidence or just luck that had drawn the drunken creatures to a place occupied by nubile females. Yet as he edged his way through the bushes and shadows he lost sight of the men again as they approached closer to Ben Culver's home.

The sound of high heeled boots kicking at Culver's door filled Smith's ears as he continued moving toward where he had last spotted the two outlaws.

Without a second thought for his own welfare, Smith leapt over the white picket fence and ran to the side wall of the house as he heard the wooden door splintering into a thousand fragments around the corner.

The females inside the house began to scream as the voice of Ben Culver began to shout at the two intruders.

The sound of two shots rang out from within the property and the female screaming grew louder. Then another gunshot echoed out into the night air.

Smith drew his other .45 and then cocked both hammers as he raced through the well maintained garden up to the gaping hole where the door had once stood. Throwing himself against the wall beside the door frame the masked man readied himself for action.

Looking within the house and through the lingering gunsmoke, Smith raised both his weapons. The sounds of Ben Culver's daughters sobbing came down from up the wide staircase where they had been forcibly dragged by the two outlaws.

Smith entered the house and stepped over the fragments of wooden splinters which had once been the door before walking slowly beside the wall. For some moments he could not see much through the black gunsmoke as he came closer and closer to the stairs.

Then his eyes narrowed over the top of the bandanna as he saw the grim sight just inside the once-pristine parlour. A parlour now sprayed in the blood of two of his closest friends. It was a vision he had expected and yet it still turned his stomach as he looked down at the blood-covered floor.

Ben Culver lay lifeless on his back beside his wife's body. He had two bullet-holes in his chest. Both had been ruthlessly slain by two of Hardin's vermin.

Smith gripped his guns in his hands, made his way to the staircase and began to ascend quietly. Like the hunter he had once been, he moved ever upward, fully aware of even the faintest sound.

It had been ten years since he had used these pistols in anger but as his fingers stroked the triggers he wanted to kill again more intensely than he had ever done before.

The noise which came echoing off the walls about him chilled him to the bone. Smith had heard many women suffering in the past but he had not heard noises like these.

Smith knew from the sound above him that the two Culver girls, Freda and Betty, had been separated by their attackers and dragged into different rooms. As he reached the top of the flight of stairs he knew these girls were to either side of him. Both bedroom doors were wide open allowing Smith to see everything that was going on.

It was a sickening sight that met his narrowed eyes as he paused between the two rooms. He trained his guns on both rooms as the masked man stood unnoticed on the carpeted landing as he tried to ignore the females' heartbreaking pleas for mercy. He waited for two clear shots. If nothing else, Smith did not want to risk missing his chosen targets and hitting either of Ben Culver's daughters.

To his right he recognized the elder, Freda, by her golden hair as she lay upon the top of a wide bed. Her dress had been thrown over her upper body and her under garments ripped from her body by her attacker. The outlaw had his pants around his ankles as he held her hair in one hand and his pistol in the other. He was thrusting himself mercilessly into the crying girl but was too close to young Freda for the masked man to dare firing.

To his left in the room closest to Smith, the other outlaw had decided he wanted something less conventional and was about to get what he wanted.

Keeping one gun aimed on the room where Freda was being raped the man with the bandanna over his face moved closer to the horror which was being inflicted on the younger Betty. What his mature eyes saw beggared belief.

The near naked female was covered in her own blood as her attacker loomed over her. As he straightened up to commit his ultimate humiliation upon the dazed and terrified Betty Culver, Smith could not wait another second.

Firing twice, he hit the outlaw through the head and neck sending his worthless carcass hurtling into a corner of the bedroom. Without even stopping to check his handiwork, Smith turned and began walking back toward the room where Freda's aggressor was turning to see who had fired the pair of deadly shots.

The sight of the tall man, whose eyes were blazing eyes between the brim of his Stetson and his bandanna, filled the drunken wretch with a horror he had never experienced before. Yet it was nothing to the pain he and his cohort had inflicted upon the daughters of Ben Culver.

'Who are you?' the outlaw's voice trembled as he tried to drag his filthy pants up to cover himself. His thighs were covered in blood, a virgin's blood. 'I asked you a question, *hombre.*'

Joe Smith had never felt such a burning fury inside his guts as he stared at the bastard before him trying to hide his sagging manhood.

'You know who I am.'

The outlaw was confused. 'Nope. Tell me.'

'I'm your executioner, you gutter slime,' Smith replied. He raised both guns at the figure who suddenly realized he was still holding one of his pistols in his own trembling hand.

As the outlaw released his grip on his pants he

moved his left hand across and fanned his gun-hammer. A bullet blasted from the outlaw's gun. Smith squeezed the triggers on both his guns in reply. A frightening volley of shots flashed like lightning across the landing in both directions.

The masked man had not missed his target.

The outlaw twisted and fell to the floor as his life came to a bloody end. The cold eyes which glared over the top of the bandanna watched impassively as the body twitched on the floor at Joe's feet. He knew the Devil would be waiting for this one, as well as the other wretched souls of Hardin's men.

He vowed to send them all there before the night was over and a new day had a chance to be born.

Over the bandanna which hid his features Joe spied a petrified creature. Smith wanted to reveal his identity to her but he knew the mask was the only protection his wife and children had from the other roaming outlaws.

A terrified Freda Culver crouched on the floor in the corner of the room, sobbing. The masked man tried not to look in her direction as he dragged the lifeless body out to the landing where Betty stood watching.

'You girls had better go hide in the cellar,' Smith said. He swallowed hard.

Betty staggered to the bedroom door and wiped the blood from her face as she looked at her sister.

Smith glanced at the pitiful figure and pointed to where Freda was crying. Betty had no idea she was near naked and covered in the outlaw's rancid residues.

'Get some clothes on, Betty. It'll be cold in the cellar. Get your sister and yourself down there and bolt the door,' Smith said as he began to walk down the staircase.

'How do you know my name?' the injured yet still beautiful creature asked. She watched the tall man with eyes that tried to thank him.

'I'll be back when my job is done.' The masked man holstered one of his guns and reloaded the other.

'But what if they ...' Betty's voice seemed to falter as she thought of what might still happen to them if this strange, quiet man should fail in his purpose.

'I promise you, I'll return.'

For some strange inexplicable reason, Betty Culver felt that the man who had saved the lives of Freda and herself would come back exactly as he promised. However many evil outlaws remained in their small town, none of them could match the gun-skills of this masked figure.

There was no more time for Smith to talk. She watched whilst he left the house as silently as he had entered.

He had thirty-eight two-legged rats to destroy.

NINE

'Don't you figure it's getting out of hand, Trent?'
Ben Franks asked as he wiped the gravy off his
mouth on to the back of his sleeve.

Hardin pushed the plate forward and stared
around the saloon at the three elderly female
prisoners he had forced to cook food for them.

'Quit grumbling, Ben,' Hardin ordered before
waving for the old women to come and remove
their plates as he pulled a long cigar from his
inside vest pocket and bit off its tip.

'There's too much shooting. It's getting out of
hand,' Franks said as he lifted his coffee cup and
sipped at the black beverage.

'You're only jealous 'coz we ain't got the energy
any more to sow our oats and join in.' Hardin
struck a match and lifted the flame to his cigar.
He inhaled the smoke and stared at the old
women who carried the dishes away. 'I figure we
couldn't even satisfy them.'

'You ought to drink some coffee, Trent,' Franks advised the man who had not slept in at least forty-eight hours.

'I'm OK,' Hardin snarled. He pushed back his chair, and got to his feet and plucked a bottle of whiskey from the bar-top. He returned to his seat. 'I figure a few shots of rye will wake me up just fine.'

Franks pulled out his pocket-watch and opened the silver lid to check the time.

'It's nearly nine.'

Hardin shrugged. A plume of smoke drifted from his lips.

'We got plenty of time before the gold train is due back, Ben. Stop fretting. The boys will be better after they've had their fun.'

'But there's far too much shooting out there,' Franks protested.

Hardin turned as yet another volley of shots echoed around the small saloon from somewhere out there in the darkness. 'Maybe they are getting a tad boisterous but once they've had their fun they'll calm down.'

'You reckon?'

'Soon we'll get them to start herding the town's citizens down to the rail-track.' Hardin pulled the cork from the neck of the whiskey bottle and spat it on to the floor.

'What?'

'That, my dear friend, is the master-stroke of

my plan.' The smile on Hardin's face as he swallowed the three fingers of whiskey widened hideously.

Ben Franks leaned forward. 'Why would we want to take people to the rail-track?'

'The train will stop if we cover the track with women and children, Ben,' Hardin crowed as he took more shots of whiskey.

'You serious?' The look of shock which overwhelmed Frank's face made Harding's grin even wider.

'I sure am.'

Hardin nodded as yet more gunshots rang out, causing him to turn and look out of the open saloon doors. For the first time this night even he began to wonder why so many guns were being fired out there on the streets.

He was right to be concerned.

The masked figure slipped back into the shadows, leaving the two dead outlaws beside the fenced-off pasture beyond the livery stable. He had given them a chance to prove they were faster than he was. A chance they had taken.

Smith had killed them both with one shot each before they had even managed to get their Colts out of their holsters. A few yards away two other outlaws lay in their own blood after taking the same challenge.

Smith emptied the spent shells from his

weapons and reloaded his guns. He continued to walk through the darkness, seeking out more of the outlaws. As he moved along the boardwalk towards the barber-shop he noticed another kicked-in door opposite. The sound which came from within the dwelling made Smith pause as yet another half-dozen of Hardin's men came around the corner directly in front of him.

One of the outlaws was triumphantly holding several female underclothes in his grubby hands and all the men laughed. The men raised their heads when they saw the tall, dark-clad, masked figure standing before them like a granite statue.

The pathetic laughter faded as all six outlaws dragged their feet to a halt and began to take in the image that was squaring up before them.

Gates Brown pushed his way between the outlaws to get a better look at the ominous man who was raising his hands above his matched Colts. For a moment Gates had a smile across his unshaven face as he assumed the tall figure must be one of their own men. Then he focused through the poor light on to the bandanna that was pulled up to just beneath the eyes.

'Pull on him, boys,' Gates screamed. He went for his own guns as his cohorts reached for their own weaponry.

Smith drew both his guns faster than any of his opponents. Instinctively he used his thumbs to cock their hammers before squeezing the triggers.

Somehow the group of outlaws managed to get some of their bullets aimed in Smith's direction as their *amigos* fell dead around them.

The boardwalk ripped apart as the guns fired into the ground from men who were falling as the deadly accuracy of the man behind the bandanna continued to pick them off, without his moving an inch in either direction.

Then the firing stopped.

Smith had emptied both his six-shooters.

As the area between them filled with the choking, dark, gunsmoke residue, Smith holstered one of his pistols and shook the spent shells from the other. He pulled six bullets from his pants pocket and slid all of them into the hot chambers of the gun.

As the gunsmoke cleared, his narrow eyes were satisfied that he had dropped every one of the men on the street. He paused to load his other pistol, then he walked straight towards the house opposite the barber-shop and the sounds of distress which drew him like a moth to a flame.

Now there were twenty-eight left.

TEN

A lantern's glowing amber light made the brass plaque on the wall gleam as Smith ran straight into the open doorway of the house. This was the home of Doc Vine and his wife, Martha. They shared their modest home with their married son Pete and his wife Ellie.

The sound of muffled screams came from above, in one of the bedrooms. The masked man was drawn in the direction of the dark stairs by the chilling sound of a female being cruelly mistreated; then, a blinding flash from a side room tore through the cool air, missing him by a few inches. The deafening sound of a rifle being fired came a split second later. Smith ducked and squinted into the blackened room.

Another Winchester shot blasted a hole in the wall above his Stetson as he fanned the hammer of his right-hand pistol, sending his defiant reply back at the mysterious rifleman. Smith could hear the noise of the carbine's mechanism being quickly cocked as he dived to the side of the doorway.

Another bullet cut through the air, leaving a red-hot trail of light in the air before it went straight through a framed painting on a far wall, bringing it crashing to the floor. Countless slivers of glass showered over the crouching masked man as he heard the sound of more men gathering angrily above him at the top of the staircase.

Smith could see nothing in the blackness.

At least six of the drunken outlaws had left what they were doing and assembled on the landing as they tried to see who and what their fellow outlaw was firing at beneath them in the hallway.

Smith could hear the sound of pistols being drawn from their holsters up at the top of the stairs. Then they began firing down their lethal lead. The air between them seemed alive with deadly fireflies but choking with the acrid aroma of gunsmoke.

The floorboards all around the masked man exploded in anger as Joe Smith rolled over and over into the blackness at the side of the stairs. He could see nothing but the red flashes which rained down on him. Smith returned another desperate shot back at the white deafening flashes above him.

Another rifle shot blasted from out of the room as Smith's eyes finally began to adjust to the total darkness whilst he kept on moving from side to side.

Pulling his other gun from its holster Joe Smith pulled both hammers back until they cocked and rested his spine against the wall before firing into the room several times.

A pitiful shriek came from the room followed by an explosive rifle blast as its owner dropped the weapon and staggered forward out into the hall.

Smith fired both his Colts again into the centre of his target and watched as the figure slumped onto the floor. Before the man wearing the bandanna over his face had time to feel any relief a bullet tore through the dark fabric of his shirt on his left shoulder sending white-hot pain burning through his body as he tumbled on to his side.

As he felt blood pulsing out of the wound on the top of his shoulder he began firing both his handguns up into the darkness above him as bullets bombarded the floor around him. The smell of burning splinters and sawdust filled his nostrils as he continued fearlessly firing up into the blackness.

At the top of the stairs another man screamed and fell headlong downward like a boulder. The body came rolling down the stairs crashing to a halt across Smith's legs. Then another lifeless outlaw fell over the balustrade and crashed on to a small wall table, turning it into matchwood within a few inches of Smith's prostrate body.

Smith scrambled feverishly back on to his knees and managed to see the image of a man running down the stairs toward him through the blinding gunsmoke firing wildly in all directions.

The masked man pulled hard on both triggers and heard the deathly gasp as the outlaw tripped and rolled over until he fell out onto the board-walk into the street.

Without a moment's hesitation, Smith started up the staircase as he felt his own blood seeping down his back from the nagging wound on his shoulder. With each step he fired as less and less lead was returned from the outlaws.

Suddenly the firing ceased. As Smith grew closer to the second floor he knew they were all dead.

As Smith reached the landing his eyes had adjusted to the darkness and he could see three bodies strewn out with his lead in them. Then he moved toward a room where a table-lamp shed a soft glow. He pushed the door open and swallowed hard at the bloodcurdling sight.

The light flickered as it illuminated the bodies of Doc Vine and his son. They had died slowly at the hands of the men who had used barber's razors on them. Smith wondered how many cuts it had taken before the carved-up bodies had died.

Martha Vine lay partly clothed on top of the room's wide bed, staring with lifeless eyes up in the direction of the place where, he thought, she must now have surely gone to. The masked man leaned over and closed her eyes with the fingers of his left hand.

She had been used by the vermin he had just exterminated. Her naked lower body bore the scars of their handiwork. Trails of blood showed she had been cut many times before she had finally sought peace in the arms of death. Joe Smith covered her body and then moved quickly back on to the landing, carrying the lamp in his free hand. He stepped over the bodies of his victims and pushed the other bedroom door open.

It was empty.

Without even taking a breath, Smith descended the stairs and stepped over the body of the man who had been using the Winchester rifle so effectively. He held the lamp through the half-open door of a room, and carefully studied every detail before him. For a second he thought the room was empty, then he heard a sound coming from behind the large desk that Doc Vine had so cherished.

Cautiously, Smith walked into the room, a lamp in one hand and a gun in the other.

When he reached the desk he rested the lamp on top of the ink-blotter. Then his narrowed eyes saw Ellie Vine, whimpering like a whipped animal, behind the desk. Her eyes were glazed and she shook where she sat in the dust, clutching her naked legs close to her chest. Even by the poor light of the lamp, Smith could see the bruises and blood which covered her flesh. It was as if every inch of her skin had cruel finger-marks upon it. Blood was trickling from her nose and mouth but she did not seem aware of her injuries.

There was a point when even the strongest mind would snap into a million pieces if tortured enough. Ellie Vine was a simple young lady who had found peace in a place most people could not even imagine. Her own soul.

'It's going to be OK, Ellie,' Smith said, trying to comfort her. But she was unaware of his presence. She heard nothing. She saw nothing. She just sat in what remained of her clothing, shaking with a fear no human should ever experience.

He wondered what he could do for her; then realized that there was nothing any man could do. Smith had seen faces such as hers many times during the Indian Wars; the faces of females who no longer seemed able to cope with the horrors of reality and sought refuge in their own insanity.

'I'll make them pay, Ellie.'

He left the lamp on the desk, walked away from the house and paused on the boardwalk doing his sums as he touched the flesh wound which was still bleeding.

Quickly he loaded his guns again as his eyes flashed around the street looking for more of Hardin's riders.

By his calculations, there were twenty-one out-laws left in Powder Springs.

Tapping his pants pockets, he knew he had just about enough bullets left, but it would be a close-run thing.

ELEVEN

Hardin stood outside the saloon with Ben Franks at his side. He finished his cigar and flicked it out into the street. He watched it bounce in the dust, sending red sparks into the darkness. Then he turned to his companion.

'Round up the boys, Ben. Something's wrong out here, very wrong.'

Franks moved closer to the outlaw leader whose face was now like stone.

'I told you there was too much damn shooting out here.'

'Yeah, you told me,' Hardin agreed as he looked around the street which held too many secrets in the dim lantern-light. Too many shadows. 'What time is it now?'

Franks fumbled the silver watch from his vest pocket and flipped open its lid. 'Getting close to midnight.'

Hardin rubbed his chin as he searched his pockets, vainly looking for another cigar.

'This don't smell right, Ben.'

'Some of these varmints must have gone, I reckon,' Franks said as he tried to spit with a mouth devoid of any moisture. 'Them folks have been taking pot shots at our boys. I bet you that's what they've been doing, Trent.'

Hardin ventured out onto the boardwalk and rested a hand against the wooden upright as his mind raced. The train would be heading through Powder Springs laden down with fresh-minted money in roughly three hours and he had to ensure that they stopped it. He wondered whether his vivid imagination was playing tricks on him; that he was just weary from lack of sleep. On the other hand, he knew the air had the aroma of gunsmoke on it. Too much gunsmoke.

'If someone has been taking wild shots at our boys, how come none of them have come here to tell me, Ben?' Hardin patted his coat-pockets as he desperately tried to find another smoke for his anxious mouth to suck upon.

Franks rubbed his whiskers. 'Yeah, it don't make a lot of sense, does it?'

'Nope. Don't make no sense at all unless whoever did the shooting has killed his targets.' Hardin shrugged as he felt the hairs on the nape of his neck rising. 'Dead men can't tell no tales.'

'That would take a gunfighter or the like,' Franks said as he moved next to the brooding man. 'I figured this town was full of nothing but regular folks.'

'You and me both, Ben.' Hardin walked along the street as his quicksilver brain tried to make sense of the problem.

Ben Franks tilted his head as he watched Hardin step off the boardwalk into the street.

'Could be our boys are just sleeping off their drink in the arms of pretty females.'

Hardin nodded as Franks joined him to walk across the wide street in the direction of the livery stables.

'You could be right but I doubt it.'

Suddenly, as they crossed in front of the schoolhouse, Hardin's keen eyes spotted something in the shadows near the dark walls of the livery stable. Swiftly, he drew both his weapons and glanced about. Then he aimed his pointed boots in the direction of the stable.

'What's wrong, Trent?' Franks asked as he tagged along beside his associate.

'Quiet,' Hardin snapped. He kept glancing round about as he proceeded toward the strange shape which had caught his eye. To the pair of ruthless outlaws it seemed suddenly as if they were on their own.

Trent Hardin stopped walking as his worst fears were realized. Looking down at the two dead outlaws who were already beginning to go stiff he felt suddenly afraid.

'I should have listened to you, Ben,' Hardin admitted. He turned and gazed into the darkness that surrounded them. 'We got trouble just like you figured.'

'But who could have done this?' Franks gulped as, reluctantly, he drew his own guns. He stared at the dark shadows that seemed to be encroaching upon them.

Hardin knelt down and studied the well-placed bullet-holes in both corpses. Then he straightened up. Whoever had done this was no clumsy amateur. This was the work of an expert.

'No fumble-brained critter did this, Ben. This was done by a gunfighter. Somebody who shouldn't be in this town.'

'Let's ride, Trent. Leave the rest of the boys here and ride.'

'I ain't yellow,' Hardin said as he stepped away from the ground which was covered in blood.

'Me neither, but this critter is damn good at killing and I don't want to end up looking down the barrel of his guns,' Franks flustered.

'We've got to get the boys together, fast,' Hardin growled angrily.

There was no argument from the man who trailed him down the street.

TWELVE

Hoot Crawford stood within the depths of his livery stable as he watched Trent Hardin and Ben Franks walking back into the heart of the town. Powder Springs was now blanketed in a creeping mist which swept along the streets, making visibility even less reliable. The old man with a spine which had buckled long ago after a lifetime of working metal on his forge, moved slowly out of the blackness towards the two bodies.

Hoot had seen the forty riders when they had arrived and was soon being led by the scruff of his neck to tend their lathered-up mounts. After hours of rubbing the animals down, he'd been forced at gunpoint to light the street lanterns. Hoot had never before had a Winchester aimed at his twisted back.

Now the pair of outlaws, who had left his spine bruised from their continuous prodding with their rifle-barrels, were dead outside the doors of his livery.

He hesitated by the stable doors, and his old eyes studied the streets around his place of business. He could not see as well as he once could, but his hearing was still as keen as ever.

As he rubbed the sweat from his wrinkled brow, he knew that the ruthless gang of outlaws had all moved away from this part of the once peaceful town. What they had left had been bodies and ruined lives. Hoot Crawford had heard the chilling screams and the deafening gunshots from his hiding-place high in the hayloft above the floor of his livery. Yet he was confused by the dead bodies before him.

Who had killed these men?

Hoot knew every man, woman and child in the small closely knit community and found it impossible to think that any of them might be capable of taking on these outlaws and beating them.

Powder Springs had no law like that of other, bigger, towns. There had never been any need, yet someone had come out of the shadows and acted like a lawman.

Who? Why?

Even if it had been daylight, Hoot knew his old eyes would still not have been able to see the face of the man who had come out of the darkness and destroyed the two outlaws as they had destroyed everything else they had come in contact with since they arrived.

The horses had been left by this vicious army of

men in his pasture and his fence was loaded with their saddles. Hoot knew the outlaws had gone for now, but the horses would bring them back.

That was a certainty. They would return.

The old stableman ventured out from the relative safety of his livery and knelt down beside the two lifeless bodies of the men who had vented their violence upon him for so many tortuous hours.

Hoot felt nothing. No anger. No happiness. Nothing.

For the life of him, Hoot could not fathom why these men had come to his town. There was no money here to speak of. There was no bank to rob. Yet they had come and killed innocent people like Lucas Green. They had despoiled countless females if the earlier screams were anything to go by.

Then he saw the four guns lying in the dust and the pair of Winchester rifles beside the bodies. For the first time since the forty killers had entered Powder Springs, he felt hope rising like sap inside his ancient body.

Without even knowing why, Hoot picked up both of the handguns, then the rifles and slipped back inside the livery stable.

Unaware that Hardin was at the other end of the town trying desperately to gather his remaining men together, Floyd Singleton and Cole Dewer led a handful of their fellow outlaws away from two of the houses on the outskirts of Powder Springs. Most of the men were still feeling the effects of their earlier drinking but none had any apologies for the atrocities they had inflicted on the innocent victims of the town. Neither did they have any idea of what had been occurring throughout Powder Springs over the past few hours. Like the rattled Hardin, they had assumed the gunfire had been nothing more than their fellow drunken cohorts letting off steam either before, during or after committing their equally vile acts.

Cole Dewer had not consumed as much liquor as the men who were following him. He was a man who preferred to smoke his hand-rolled cigarettes. Even females, however attractive, did not tempt him as much as a pouch of tobacco and gummed papers. His only concern in life was to keep his matches dry.

Yet he had been with the other outlaws as they drank and raped their way through the houses of the small town. He seemed to take pleasure in seeing others enjoying themselves far more than trying to emulate their pleasures himself.

Some said he was nothing more than a thief who rode from one town to the next with a smouldering cigarette in the corner of his mouth. There were those who said that they had never seen the man use his weaponry. Trent Hardin had kept

Cole Dewer in his gang for one reason only; he was the only man who could be relied upon to hit what he aimed at with both his handguns and his Winchester.

Men like Dewer were valuable and Hardin knew it.

'It's gone a mite quiet,' said one of the outlaws trailing behind Dewer and Singleton. He pointed his carbine up in the air and squeezed its trigger. The shot made each of the outlaws jump with the exception of cold-blooded Dewer. It took more than a volley from a carbine to make him break into a sweat. That was not his way.

The group of men stopped and turned to face the grinning young outlaw who was clutching his rifle across his chest.

'Was you born stupid or did you have to practise, Clem?' Dewer asked. He sucked the last of the smoke from his cigarette before dropping the quarter-inch of butt on to the ground and extinguishing its fire with his boot-heel.

The young outlaw's face suddenly went pale as he stared at the older, more lethal Dewer, who pulled out his cigarette-pouch from his vest pocket and proceeded to make a fresh quirly.

'You shouldn't talk to me like that, Cole,' said Clem Masters, as his fingers twitched on the Winchester's trigger. Masters cocked the rifle and stared through his matted hair at the calm Dewer, who he was already licking the gummed paper of his cigarette whilst the pouch hung from his teeth by its pull-string.

'You must be drunker than even I thought you was, Clem,' Dewer said. He pushed the cigarette into his mouth and struck a match along his belt-buckle. He raised the flame to the quirly.

'Better than being an old man like you, Cole.' Masters began to lower his rifle-barrel in the direction of the group of outlaws before him. He was drunk. Young and drunk, and it did not mix.

Floyd Singleton pushed some of the outlaws off the boardwalk into the street as he realized what was happening. He had seen the lethal Dewer in action many times and knew the man's fuse was already burning.

'Take it easy, boys,' pleaded Singleton drunk-enly.

'Shut the hell up, Floyd,' said Masters. He trained the carbine straight at Cole Dewer who was deeply inhaling the smoke of his cigarette. He looked straight into the youngster's eyes.

'Yeah, shut up, Floyd. Clem here wants to kill me,' said Dewer through a cloud of smoke. 'I figure it's his right to try.'

'Don't be a fool, Clem. Cole is fast. Real fast,' warned Singleton, keeping the other men behind him.

Suddenly, as the young outlaw stared along the barrel of his rifle he saw, over Cole Dewar's shoulder, the figure of a masked man walking towards them through the mist. Masters blinked hard several times. He wondered if he was imagining the awesome sight.

'Do you believe in ghosts, Cole?' Masters asked, his voice fragmenting.

'What the hell you talking about, Clem?' Dewer asked, squaring up to the confused Masters.

Clem Masters lowered the rifle and then staggered towards Dewer, screwing up his drunken eyes, trying to see more clearly. It was not an easy task as the midnight mist swirled about them.

'Turn around, Cole. Take a look at that man.'

Dewer turned his head cautiously. Then he saw a man with a dark bandanna pulled up over his face standing with his hands hovering above the two gun grips.

'What in tarnation?'

Floyd Singleton joined the two outlaws as the other men all began pointing in Joe Smith's direction. While the mist continued to come and go between themselves and the defiant masked Smith, he did truly seem almost ghostlike to the drunken outlaws.

But not to Dewer.

'Is there a man down there wearing a mask, Cole?' Clem Masters asked as he felt the whiskey inside him beginning to turn mean.

'Sure is, Clem. That's no ghost. That's a living breathing human being,' Dewer replied. He turned slowly around to face the figure who was standing less than a hundred feet away from them.

'Who is it?' a voice asked.

'Ain't one of our boys,' another voice chipped in.

'What's he want?' Clem Masters coughed as he felt the whiskey finally beginning to force its way back up.

None of the outlaws answered the questions as the youngest of their group fell over a hitching rail and began to vomit noisily.

Cole Dewer raised one of his arms and pointed to the wide street.

'Fan out, boys. I figure this critter means business.'

The men began to walk across the dimly illuminated street in a drawn-out line while they watched the masked man also walk to the centre of the wide street.

'What do you want, masked man?' Dewer called out. He began to flex his fingers above his guns.

Joe Smith said nothing but lowered his head and, below the rim of his hat, riveted his eyes on the men. Even in the poor light and teasing mist he could see every one of them.

The hapless Clem Masters tottered into the street clutching his rifle, after leaving the entire contents of his stomach beside the hitching rail.

'What's happening, Cole?' Masters asked, swaying on his high-heeled boots.

'Reckon it's a show-down, boy,' said Dewer as he

sucked smoke continually from the quickly shrinking cigarette between his dry lips. 'This critter seems to want burying.'

'You boys ready to die?' Smith shouted out at the men who faced him in various degrees of dishevelled readiness.

'Die?' Singleton repeated the word anxiously.

Dewer stepped forward.

'You ain't killing nobody tonight, stranger.'

Smith raised his hands over the grips of his matched Colts.

'Cole Dewer. Wanted dead or alive, as I recall.'

Dewer suddenly recognized the voice which came from behind the dark bandanna. It had been fifteen years but he still knew the voice.

'But you're dead,' said Cole Dewer, as he stared at the familiar gunbelt and the guns. A shooting-rig he had good cause to remember. 'You've been dead for years.'

'Now I'm back from the dead, Dewer,' drawled Smith as he took one step closer to his opponents.

Dewer glanced at Clem Masters before returning his keen eyes to the mysterious masked figure.

'I'm starting to think young Clem was right. This is a ghost.'

As the outlaws all stepped forward, Clem Masters raised his Winchester and aimed in the direction of the man he could only just see through the swimming fog that filled his eyes. A

fog far thicker than the natural one which continued to swirl around the town's streets.

'Don't shoot,' Singleton shouted at the youngest
member of their group. Dewer looked back at
Masters.

'No, Clem.'

It was too late. Masters tugged on the trigger
and fired the rifle. The rebound sent him staggering backward like someone who had been kicked
by a mule.

As the bullet passed within a whisker of him,
Smith drew both his guns.

Dewer swore angrily at the youngster but still
managed to get both his guns out of their holsters
a fraction of a second after their masked foe drew.
The rest of the outlaws all began pulling their
weapons out of their leather holsters as the lead
started to fly.

A well-placed shot from Dewer glanced off one
of Joe Smith's ribs sending him down on to one
knee as he continued returning fire. The black
smoke from the pistols began to fill the distance
between them as it mixed with the foggy haze.
Seeing Smith on one knee, Cole Dewer came running forward, firing his guns in an attempt to finish the job quickly.

The masked man fired twice into the advancing
outlaw, sending him crashing face down into the
ground at his side.

Clem Masters had managed to cock his rifle

again and was coming straight at the kneeling man. Smith felled him with one deadly shot as Singleton tried desperately to hit his target with both guns blazing. Smith emptied one revolver into him before raising his left-hand gun and finishing the remainder of the men who had tried to use Singleton as a shield to get closer to the kneeling masked man.

Joe Smith managed to get back on his feet as he felt the blood running down his side. Now he was bleeding in two different places and it hurt.

It hurt bad.

Holstering his empty gun, Smith touched his side and felt the deep chunk of flesh and bone that Dewer's shot had carved out of his side. It was bleeding badly.

He stepped over the body of Cole Dewer, bent over and plucked the box of matches from the outlaw's vest pocket. He knew that the dead outlaw had suddenly recognized his voice and shooting rig, when earlier he had failed to even give him a second look when they had met inside the café.

As Joe Smith walked into the blackness of an alley he thought about the men he had defeated over the past few hours and knew there had to be fewer than ten left alive in Powder Springs.

One of them was Trent Hardin. The biggest fish of them all.

It was only the thought of finally bringing

Hardin to justice that kept the tall man focused on the chore ahead.

Leaning against a wall in the alley, Smith pulled out a bullet from his pants pocket and lowered his bandanna. The wound was losing too much blood and he knew he had to do something drastic if he were going to survive. Putting a bullet between his teeth he prised it apart.

He spat out the powder from the lead ball, and pulled his shirt away from his wound. He carefully poured the black powder from the cartridge over the bleeding hole. It stung like a thousand hornets as he dropped the empty brass casing on to the ground at his feet.

Then he pulled one of Cole Dewer's prized matches out of its box and ran a thumbnail over its tip. As the flame flared he touched the gunpowder to his wound until it exploded in a blinding flash. The smell of burning flesh filled his nostrils and he found himself on his knees. For a few moments he just knelt as the pain gradually eased. Using his bandanna to wipe away the tears from his eyes he carefully touched the wound. It was no longer bleeding.

He had bought himself some time.

Now he at least would not die from losing his life's blood.

He rose to his feet and tucked his shirt back into his pants. He raised his bandanna over his face until only his eyes were visible.

Having loaded his empty guns again, he began making his way through the dark alley in search of what remained of the forty riders.

Smith would not quit now. Not until he was face to face with the evil genius known as Trent Hardin. This time he would finish it.

THIRTEEN

Trent Hardin stood amid the bodies of his half-dozen men, trying to grasp the situation as Ben Franks walked silently around trying vainly to find at least one of them alive. Hardin had managed to gather a pathetic twelve of their original gang together before discovering Cole Dewer and his companions lying lifeless in the mist-shrouded street.

Hardin and Franks had heard the dramatic gun battle while they were finding their wayward men in various beds in several houses as they planted their demon seeds wherever they wished. Like their equally obnoxious cohorts, the dozen remaining outlaws had taken what they wanted and savaged whoever had objected to their perversion. To these mainly youthful outlaws it was all just a barrel of laughs. To Hardin and the increasingly concerned Franks, it was far more serious.

To Hardin's and Franks' dismay, they had found a number of members of their gang dead in the dark lonely shadows long before they had managed to gather the living ones.

Only the unscrupulous Spangler Brough and one of his favourite cohorts, Dan Gibson, had eluded the frantic search by Hardin and Franks as they had moved through the town, tripping over the bodies of their fellow outlaws. Wherever they were and whatever they were doing, neither Hardin nor Franks could locate them.

They had however found far too many bodies of their missing men. Bodies which all showed they had been dispatched with an expertise that chilled even the cold hearts of Hardin and company.

'Spangler and Dan must be dead too,' said Ben Franks as he plucked ammunition from the bodies of the dead men to fill his pockets.

'Most likely,' Hardin responded, standing in the centre of where his best men had fallen.

Hardin was brooding over his losses. This was not the way it was meant to happen. He had come here with an army of men and the best plan he had ever devised and yet he was now standing with only a baker's dozen of gunmen left. Sweat rolled down from beneath the band of his hat, although the night air was cold and biting.

Inhaling deeply, Trent Hardin refused to face Franks or any of the other outlaws who stood clutching their weaponry. Their nervous eyes stared all around them, waiting for death to attack from every shadow. He had to try to make sense of this situation quickly if his plan were still to work.

Hardin always clad in black leather, had ridden too many miles to rob the bullion train at this unique spot, to allow anyone or anything to stop him. Yet he knew that the thirteen souls remaining beside him were ready to cut and run. He had to try and turn their fears around and make them angry enough to stand up to their mysterious foe or foes.

Hardin walked to where Dewer still lay and looked down at the corpse lying in a huge pool of blood. This had been his top gun and the only one who ever managed to outdraw him, yet Dewer was dead and Hardin could not figure out why.

'Who the hell are we up against, Ben?'

Franks paced towards the brooding Hardin.

'I figure we better get our horses and ride, Trent. This ain't going to plan and I'm scared.'

Hardin's eyes flashed up at the face which was sweating even more than his own. He knew this was the general mood of his remaining men and he had to turn it around.

'Quit? There are still fourteen of us left. That's a mighty big gang and no mistake.'

The twelve other outlaws moved to the two men who were standing toe to toe, looking into each other's faces.

'Ben's right, boss,' one of the men said.

Hardin lifted his gun and aimed at the face of the outlaw as he fought with his own instincts to kill the voice which dared to question his authority.

'Say that again, boy.'

The outlaw shook his head. 'I don't want to die, boss.'

Franks moved closer to Hardin and spoke into the man's ear.

'We can't afford to kill our own, Trent. There's some critter out there who's better at it than we are.'

Hardin lowered his gun and shrugged. 'The plan could still work if we keep together. My plan only needed forty men to gain control of this town. We've done that already. We are still a big enough bunch to take the train.'

'But someone is picking us off, Trent.' Franks coughed nervously.

'Our boys have only been picked off when they split up into small groups,' Hardin said thoughtfully.

'Maybe the critter bushwhacked them?' another of the younger men suggested.

Franks gripped Hardin's shoulder.

'Yeah, that's it. All our boys have been dry-gulched by some snivelling coward.'

Hardin started to smile. 'True. Only a bushwhacker could have managed to get the drop on

Cole. Cole Dewer was the best gunhand I ever seen and I've seen them all.'

'Maybe there's more than one of them picking us off,' another of the outlaws said as they all began to walk away from the scene of carnage. 'Could be a whole gang.'

'I bet it is a gang,' said Hardin, and nodded as he began to feel that there was still a chance of his plan to rob the north-bound train actually succeeding now that he had managed to get his gang thinking.

'Could be some varmints from one of them ranches we passed on the way here,' Franks suggested.

'Yeah, that sort of makes sense. A bunch of back-shooters off a farm or something have been killing our boys.' Hardin was beginning to feel a lot better as they headed through the mist back in the direction of the saloon and the rail-track.

'Stinkin' cowards,' one of the outlaws spat as the others all began to grunt in agreement.

'Yeah, stinkin' cowards.' Hardin began to toy with one of his pistols as he wondered who it was out there in the darkness, killing his men. 'They wouldn't have the guts to face us square on like real men. We just have to stick together and they'll keep away from us and our guns.'

The young outlaws all seemed to be getting fired up by the sheer enthusiasm of their clever leader. They knew he would not allow anyone to spoil his plan to hold up the train. Not as the time was getting close to when it was due back in Powder Springs.

'So we ain't quiting this town?' Franks checked with Trent Hardin.

'Nope,' said Hardin, with a renewed sense of his own power and invincibility. 'We're sticking to the plan just the way I worked it out, Ben.'

'So we're still going to rob the train?'

'You bet.'

'I thought so.' Franks sighed as he walked beside the leader of their gang who was trying to find another cigar somewhere in his many pockets.

'What time is it now, Ben?' Hardin asked as they walked defiantly down the middle of the wide street. They were still a force to be reckoned with by anyone's standards, and he knew it.

Ben Franks took his watch out of his pocket and knew there was no chance they would be riding out of Powder Springs until they had completed the job which had brought them here to the back of beyond.

'Twenty before one.'

'Less than two hours,' Hardin said. 'Soon we'll start rounding up the women and children, boys.'

Franks' face froze when he thought about tying people across the rail-tracks.

'Maybe we ought to just block the track so the train has to stop, Trent,' he suggested.

'I like my idea better.'

Ben Franks snapped the silver cover of his watch shut and slid it back in his pocket. He was not happy about any of this but had no idea how to stop it.

'We ain't beaten yet by a long chalk, boys,' Hardin said as he led the thirteen men into the swirling mist back in the direction of the saloon.

FOURTEEN

Hoot Crawford had remained hiding up in his hay-loft with the salvaged handguns and rifles for nearly an hour. From his high vantage-point he should have been able to see everything there was to see in Powder Springs, but the combination of darkness and seventy-year-old eyes made it a futile venture.

He had seen blurred images which had taunted him. A shimmering figure which had out drawn the two outlaws below the hay-loft yet he had no idea of what the man had looked like.

The cold fog came and went on the temperamental breeze with unnerving regularity. One moment the street was clear and the next it disappeared from view.

Hoot Crawford was tired but knew he dare not sleep for fear of being discovered by the ruthless gang who were still out there somewhere in the small town. He had been kicked and prodded with long rifle-barrels throughout the day and did not relish it happening again whilst he slept.

Why he had taken the weapons from the two dead outlaws was still a mystery to the old livery man. Yet he felt safer now as he clutched on to one of the fully loaded Winchesters. The whispering of the cold night air as it tossed the swirling mist about the stable filled his old ears again as he saw the bunch of more than a dozen heavily armed figures marching past one of the glowing street-lanterns a few hundred yards away. They were heading in the direction of the well-lit saloon.

Although Hoot's eyes could not make out any detail, he knew that only the hell-bent gang could muster a group of such numbers. Yet, to the owner of the stable, there seemed fewer of them now than earlier.

Hoot assumed that this group of outlaws was just part of the greater army with which Hardin had entered town; the others would show up soon to join them.

Now they were gathering like coyotes after a kill. Hoot knew he ought to do something.

Something which would wipe the smiles off their faces.

But what?

He had four pistols and two carbine rifles. In the right hands the townspeople might be able to fight. But who in all of Powder Springs could even use a gun, let alone hit what they were aiming at?

110

As far as the old man knew, all the citizens of the small town were as useless as he was when it came to firearms. Nobody in Powder Springs even wore a gun, unlike most towns he had lived in during his long life. There had never been any reason to learn to shoot until today. Now it was far too late to learn.

Yet somebody had killed those outlaws.

As Hoot Crawford rolled away from the loft window and found his corncob pipe in his vest-pocket he heard a noise. For a moment he thought it was a rat. Then he knew it was the sound of a man in high-heeled boots walking across the sod floor of his livery stable below him.

Sticking his pipe in his toothless mouth, he clutched one of the Winchester rifles and waited between the bales of hay. His keen hearing told him someone was stalking stealthily around the empty stable directly beneath him.

Hoot Crawford's heart began to pound like a freight-train as he heard the hands and boots of the man coming up his ladder. The man was climbing up to the hay loft slowly.

As the old man tried to aim the long heavy weapon at the point where the ladder reached the loft, he felt terror racing through his timeworn body. His hands began to shake with a mixture of fear and the unaccustomed weight of the long-barrelled carbine.

Was it one of the outlaws?

Had they decided to kill him the way they had killed Lucas Green only minutes after arriving in town?

Hoot clutched the rifle and wondered whether his time had finally come to strap on wings and pluck a harp.

Maybe they had decided he had killed the two men outside his stables and had come to dish out punishment. A thousand questions tore through his mind when he saw the blurred outline of the Stetson appear over the edge of the loft.

As he waited in the darkness between two bales of hay, Hoot knew he could not squeeze the trigger. He had lived three-score years and ten without ever firing any sort of weapon.

Whatever fate or punishment awaited him when the man reached his hiding-place, he would have to take it. He could not shoot another living creature.

Then, helped by the faint starlight which filtered through the open hayloft door and illuminated the hayloft, he managed to focus his weak eyes on what was beneath the hat.

What he saw filled him with even more terror.

The eyes which glinted in the poor light saw him. Eyes which were the only part of the face not hidden by the hat and the bandanna which was pulled up to the bridge of his nose.

'Goddam,' Hoot said softly. He felt the rifle slip from his fingers as he froze with fright at the

112

sight of the man who clambered up on to the loft platform.

For a moment the two men just looked at each other in the pale light of the stars that managed to penegrate the loft.

'Take it easy, Hoot,' the familiar voice told him quietly as the figure crawled toward him.

'Joe?' Hoot instantly recognized the voice of the man he knew only as the town baker.

Smith pulled the mask off his face and forced a smile through the pain which still racked his body from his gunshot wounds.

'It's only me, Hoot. Take it easy.'

The livery-man crawled toward the sighing figure who was leaning against a wooden joist in obvious distress.

'So it was you who gunned down them critters?'

'Yeah, it was me,' Smith admitted. He leaned to one side and stared out of the loft window at the brightly illuminated saloon a few hundred yards away.

'Where did you get the fancy guns and belt, son?'

'It's a long story.'

Hoot suddenly noticed the torn shirt and the dried blood which covered his side.

'You're hurt, boy.'

Smith nodded. 'Got any water up here, Hoot? I got me a powerful thirst.'

'Sure enough, Joe. I got me a full canteen.' Hoot

reached behind the bale of hay and picked up a full canteen from beside the handguns. 'Drink it all if you've a mind, I can always get more from the pump out in the pasture.'

Unscrewing the stopper slowly, Joe Smith put the canteen to his lips and swallowed.

'Who shot you?'

'I didn't get introduced to the first swine who winged my shoulder but the one who shot half my rib off was called Cole Dewer,' Smith said. He took another look drink. 'He was faster than I figured but I got lucky and killed him.'

'I don't understand, Joe,' said Hoot, edging close. 'I never even knew you could use a gun let alone take on men like these killers.'

Joe Smith gasped as he felt the water refreshing him.

'I was once a gunfighter, Hoot. I even worked as a lawman for a while before ending up as a bounty-hunter.'

Hoot Crawford could not conceal his surprise at hearing this statement.

'You were a bounty-hunter? Hunting men down for the price on their heads?'

Smith rested the canteen on his lap. 'Yeah. A lousy bounty-hunter who killed to get the reward money. Then one day, when I was hunting down a ruthless outlaw, I happened to ride into Powder Springs. At first I thought it might be one of them outlaw hide-outs, but then I met all of you folks. I met Lucas and I met his daughter Olive.'

'You always said you were just a baker, boy,' Hoot said as he listened keenly.

'I lied. My pa had been a baker and I knew everything there was to know about the job. I just kind of pretended to be a simple baker. I did it so I could stay here with Olive.'

'You quit hunting men to stay with her?'

'She was worth it.' Smith took another mouthful of water and then crawled closer to the loft opening and stared out at the saloon bathed in lamplight. 'I quit and I'm glad. Besides, when you hunt down and kill enough folks, you end up with a lot of enemies who want to kill you. I was famous. I had a dozen or more outlaws willing to pay good money to see me end up on boot hill with their friends.'

Hoot moved to Smith's side. He was resting his elbows on a bale of hay, drinking the last of the water in the canteen.

'Who are these men who came here, Joe?'

Smith glanced at his old friend. 'The leader's named Trent Hardin, Hoot. He's a darn smart planner of robberies and he ain't got a moral bone in his body.'

'You know him?'

'He was the man I was trailing all those years ago when I first discovered Powder Springs,' Smith said thoughtfully. 'I reckon if I had not stayed here but kept after him, none of what has happened here today would have occurred.'

'How come?'

'Because I'd have caught and killed the critter,' Smith said. His eyes narrowed and his expression hardened. 'All this is my fault for not killing him when I had the chance all those years ago.'

'None of this is your fault, Joe.' Hoot rested a hand on the younger man's arm.

'It is. I let him get away so I could pretend to be Joe Smith and have an easy life.' Smith shook his head and got up on one knee. 'Everyone who has been hurt and killed in Powder Springs today has me to thank, Hoot.'

There was nothing the old man could say which would rid his friend of the guilt which was eating him alive. But he could help him. Whether or not he wanted it, Hoot Crawford was determined to help him.

FIFTEEN

'Did you hear that?' Spangler Brough turned to the figure beside him as they ducked through the fence-poles and entered the pasture beside the livery stable. It was still dark in Powder Springs, which made both men less than happy when they moved along the fence-poles towards the big building. Forty saddles and tack straddled the top of the fence-poles where Hoot Crawford had placed them.

Dan Gibson held out a hand to stop Brough and gazed up at the wall of the stable. He had heard the voices again and was getting more and more disquieted by them.

'I hear talking, Spangler.'

'Me too,' Brough said. He looked around the horses, trying to recognize his own mount.

The pair of outlaws had been having their fun in much the same manner as their cohorts when they had heard the gunfire which had signalled

117

the end of Cole Dewer and his cronies. From that moment on the two men had been trying to locate the gunfighter or gunfighters.

After more than thirty minutes of looking, they had only found bodies. Dozens of bodies. The corpses of their fellow outlaws seemed to fill every shadowy corner of the mist-filled streets.

Being a man of less than heroic courage, Spangler Brough had decided that whoever had been killing Trent Hardin's men was damn good with his guns and not a man he himself wished to encounter. It had not taken much to persuade Dan Gibson that they ought to get their horses and ride as far away from this small town as possible.

As they had headed for the livery stable and found more and more of their fellow gang members lying dead, they both began to realize that Hardin posed an equal danger to them. He wanted to execute his plan to rob the bullion train, at all costs. Nothing would deter him from achieving this goal. To Brough and Gibson, this heist would be just as dangerous as meeting the mysterious avenger.

Using the darkened alleys to ensure they did not encounter Hardin and the remaining outlaws, Brough and Gibson had managed to reach the pasture without being noticed by anyone. This in itself was an achievement.

'Who do you figure that's talking, Spangler?'

Gibson asked as he moved slowly along the fence trying to recognize his own saddle amongst so many similar rigs.

Brough shook his head as he too tried to locate his own saddle. They came closer and closer to the livery building.

'Could be that old livery man gabbing.'

'But who's he talking to?'

Spangler Brough bit his lip. 'Yeah, who the hell would he be talking to?'

Gibson reached the last saddle next to the wall of the livery stable and sighed in frustration as he realized that he must have missed his own custom-built rig somewhere along the fencing.

With only the light of a few dim street-lanterns and a handful of stars above their heads, it was no easy task to recognize something you would know immediately in daylight. The swirling mist did not help either.

'Damn. I've missed my saddle, Spangler,' Gibson said in a low voice intended to reach only one pair of ears. He had no stomach for wasting even more time by moving back along the fence-pole again trying to find his handmade saddle.

Spangler Brough rested his knuckles on his hips above his gun-grips and stared at the forty restless animals as they milled around the lush pasture.

'You see our horses?'

'Nope,' said Gibson. He was drawn to the water-

119

trough and the pump set against the wall. He could still hear two men's voices, talking in muffled tones, coming from up high inside the livery stable.

Brough walked to his side.

'What's wrong?'

'Listen.' Gibson pointed up at the high wall. The voices drifted over them tauntingly. 'They must be up in the hay-loft, Spangler.'

Brough shrugged and leaned closer to the ear of his friend.

'Let's find our saddles and then our horses before Hardin finds us and makes us join him and the rest of the gang.'

Gibson seemed less than interested in anything Brough was saying. He seemed drawn to the sound of the two men talking above them in the loft of the stable.

'I wanna find out who's doing all the talking, Spangler.'

Brough's face went even grimmer than usual. 'What? Are you crazy, Dan? What if it's the critter whose been killing all our buddies?'

Gibson drew one of his Colts and checked it before beginning the long walk to the rear of the livery building with Spangler Brough on his heels.

'Hold up, you dang fool.'

Gibson turned and stared at the troubled face behind him.

'You find our saddles and cut out our horses, Spangler. I'll not be long.'

Brough grabbed the shoulder of his hotter-blooded companion.

'Think, boy. Think. If it is the gunfighter up there talking with the old man, you'll have to shoot him.'

'Yep. I figured that already.' Gibson stared hard into the other's face; the face of a man who no longer liked to take risks but preferred the safer ground in all situations.

'Even if you kill the bastard, Hardin will be down on us faster than a bear on a honey-pot.' Spanger Brough was using all his powers of persuasion to restrain the stronger man beside him. 'If that happens, we'll have to stay with Hardin and probably get ourselves killed when the train comes back from the mint.'

Gibson lowered his head and thought about the words which were coming at him fast and straight. Words which made him think and made him angry because he knew they were correct.

'You figure we should cut and run?'

'Damn right, Dan. They bury heroes around this town,' Spangler said. He stared at the group of mounts close to them and began to focus his eyes on the large creatures as they nervously milled around the two men. 'I ain't ever wanted to be a hero.'

Gibson nodded and was about to follow the

older man when a sharp noise came from within the livery stable. It was the sound of a wooden ladder groaning under the weight of someone stepping on to it and starting to descend.

Without knowing why, Dan Gibson pulled away from Brough. He ran round the back of the stable to its rear door and entered.

As Gibson staggered excitedly into the heart of the large building he caught sight of the figure clad all in dark clothing half-way down the stout ladder. The young outlaw could hardly believe his luck.

He raised his gun as he closed in and called up to Joe Smith.

'Hold it right there, mister.'

Joe Smith froze on the ladder and turned his head round to face the young outlaw who had his gun trained on him. A gun which he cocked eagerly with his thumb.

Dan Gibson's eyes could not believe the sight which met them as he focused on the masked face.

'What in tarnation are you meant to be?' Gibson asked in total confusion. Outlaws wore masks over their faces, not do-gooders. This man had to be an outlaw, but what was an outlaw doing here? Hardin had brought an army of outlaws to Powder Springs, but not this one. 'Who the hell are you, mister?'

There was a long chilling silence.

Smith leaned away from the ladder until he

was holding on with only one hand. He stared down on the bewildered Gibson. For a few seconds he just hovered over him, saying nothing at all. Then, he released his grip and dropped like a stone on to the bewildered youngster.

The pair crashed into the ground. Both wrestled like crazed animals in the darkness as they tried desperately to gain the upper hand. Smith felt a punch hitting his jaw but he could not feel any pain as he returned his own clenched fist with twice as much venom into the face of Gibson.

The outlaw went limp as Smith crashed two further blows into his head before staggering to his feet again. He was winded and had to hold on to the loft ladder for a few moments as he tried to clear his head.

'Easy, boy.' The voice of Spangler Brough came from behind him like a hissing sidewinder.

Joe Smith turned his masked face and glared at the figure who was holding a gun on him and cautiously edging closer.

'You got the drop on me,' Smith admitted in a hushed tone. He stared at the gun before looking up at the face of its owner.

'A masked man?' Spangler Brough seemed to question his own eyes as he drew closer to the breathless Smith, who still held on to the ladder as if afraid he might collapse if he let go.

'Don't look so surprised, mister. In your line of work I figure you must have seen quite a number of masked men.' Smith tried to think of a way out of this situation but he was hurting from his injuries and the hand that gripped the cocked pistol was firm and unshaking. This man would not miss should he pull the trigger. This man probably never missed anything he aimed at.

'Who are you?' Brough could not control his curiosity.

'Just a man who happens to be a tad shy.'

Brough laughed. 'Peel that bandanna down and let me see your face.'

Smith's eyes narrowed. 'You that interested?'

'Do it.' Brough's voice suddenly changed and he raised the barrel of the gun so that it was aiming straight at Smith's middle.

Without saying another word, Smith raised his left hand and pulled the bandanna until it fell away, revealing his features.

'Satisfied?'

'The baker.' Brough seemed totally confused by the sight which confronted him. 'You're the baker who picked up the old man after Hardin shot him. I don't get it. How come you are wearing such a fancy gunbelt? Only professionals sport that sort of rig.'

Suddenly there was a sound from the loft. Brough looked upward just in time to see the gleaming prongs of a pitchfork leaving Hoot Crawford's hand like a spear. With lethal accuracy it embedded itself deeply into the outlaw's chest.

Brough tottered back on his heels and dropped his gun as he tried frantically to pull the metal prongs out of his chest. As Spangler Brough sank to his knees blood began to pour from the corners of his mouth. The outlaw was dead as he rolled over on to his side still holding the wooden handle of the pitchfork.

Smith watched Hoot Crawford climb down the ladder.

'Much obliged, Hoot.'

'You need help, Joe.'

Smith pulled his bandanna back over his face. He knew the old man was right. He could not continue his crusade alone.

SIXTEEN

Trent Hardin had finished the better part of a bottle of whiskey. Now he glared into the long mirror behind the bar of the saloon, watching his men brooding behind him. They had drunk their share of the small town's meagre supplies and it had cost them dearly. Hardin was not going to allow them to do anything but sober up before the train rolled back through Powder Springs. None of those who remained of his gang had been allowed to drink anything but black coffee since they had arrived back at the saloon.

A cocked Colt .45 lying on the bar beside his right hand ensured that the nervous men would not question his orders. Only the silent Ben Franks seemed happy to sip at the black beverage without complaining.

The time to put the final piece of Hardin's jigsaw puzzle into place was drawing near.

Hardin knew this was his most ambitious plan

to date, but in many ways it was far simpler than robbing a bank. There were many ways to stop the train. They could have ripped up the tracks and allowed the engine to derail itself. He had considered this when the idea had first germinated in his fertile brain, but he knew what carnage that would cause. There was also the unpredictability of even a simple train wreck. Where would the carriages end up once the train crashed?

There was the possibility they might end up in such a way that his men could not gain access to the gold coins. He had seen flat cars after some train wrecks which stood on end, defying every natural law in the book.

Hardin swallowed the throat-burning rye and set his glass down for the last time. He had to stick with his original plan however much it made Ben Franks frown.

'What's the time now, Ben?'

'Two.'

Hardin nodded and turned to face the group of sorrowful-looking men.

'We've got an hour to do this right. It ain't going to be easy because the varmint who's been picking us off is still out there someplace.' Hardin slid his gun into its holster and paced into the centre of the saloon. 'I figure we have to keep together in large enough groups to scare this bushwhacker off.'

The men rose from their chairs and gathered

around their leader. None seemed to have the guts to say anything which might bring Hardin's wrath down on them. They had to go along with him because there was no other way.

'So what's first?' Franks asked as he finished his coffee and put the cup down on the bar-top.

Hardin rubbed his chin and stared straight into the face of Franks.

'You take four men down to the livery and get all our horses saddled up, Ben.'

It seemed a strange order considering there were now only fourteen of the outlaws left.

'All forty of them?' Franks queried.

'Yep. All forty of them.' Hardin nodded. 'I figure we can use all the spare mounts to carry away all the fresh-minted money we are going to get.'

Ben Franks shrugged. 'What about you and the rest of the boys, Trent?'

'We're going to rouse up all the females and children from their beds and head them off down to the rail track, Ben.' There was an evil in the tone of Hardin's words which did not sit well on the shoulders of Franks. He tried but failed to conceal his distaste.

'You still figuring on using females and kids to stop the train, Trent?' Ben Franks sighed heavily; the words made his mouth dry.

'It'll work.'

'I guess it will.'

Hardin placed a hand on Franks' shoulder.

129

'We'll light a bonfire so the train engineer will see them before he ploughs on through, Ben. The train will stop. Think about it, it has to stop.'

Franks swallowed hard. 'I sure hope you're right.'

'I am right, Ben. No train-driver would run his engine over women and children.'

Ben Franks pointed to four of the men who were closest and led them out of the saloon into the eddying mist which seemed to be getting even thicker and colder as the night progressed. He had not wished to continue talking with the man he had once respected for his genius.

As Franks led the four outlaws down the street in the direction of the livery stables he could not think of anything but the image of helpless children being used so fearfully.

'What if the train don't stop, Ben?' one of the young outlaws behind him asked as they crossed the wide misty street.

'Gonna be an awful mess, son,' came the simple reply.

SEVENTEEN

Swirling icy mist hung a few feet above the ground as the five heavily armed men strode down the centre of the eerily dark street towards the livery stable. It was an unusually anxious Ben Franks who led the four younger outlaws towards their goal.

Franks checked his pocket-watch for the umpteenth time and tried to rid his mind of what lay ahead for their depleted band, but it was impossible. He stepped on to the narrow boardwalk which led to the livery stable and cast a concerned glance over his shoulder in the direction of the saloon. He saw Hardin leading his larger group of men towards the nearest houses, where he would find the women and children he wanted to tether to the gleaming rail track.

Franks' five men moved silently along the boardwalk, then stepped down on to the frost covered ground in front of the livery. The fog seemed to grow thicker around the building and the sound of nervous horses filled the men's ears when they reached the wide-open doors.

For a moment Franks paused and stared along the dimly illuminated street, as if wondering where their mysterious adversary might be hiding. As he led his four followers through the open doors into the huge dark interior, he suddenly felt a terrifying chill overwhelm him.

All four outlaws stopped behind Franks as he stood observing the scene before them.

'What's wrong, Ben?' a voice asked.

Franks could feel his heart pounding as his eyes focused upon the two bodies resting at the foot of the loft ladder a mere twenty feet ahead of them. It was dark inside the stables but even the faint street-lights reached the bodies which lay where they had died.

'I hope you boys have your guns drawn,' the nervous outlaw said as he moved forward towards the ladder. Franks knew there was a possibility that this might be a trap to claim yet another five of Hardin's men. With every step he kept his cocked Colt trained on the bodies, just in case.

As Franks drew closer to their fallen comrades, each of the men behind his sweating spine hauled his handguns from his holster.

Cautiously the five figures walked to the pair of dead outlaws. Their wide eyes flashed from one shadow to the next as the men waited for blazing guns to claim their lives as well.

Franks knelt down and turned over the body of Dan Gibson. At first he seemed unable to work out how the outlaw had died. Then his fingers round a sharp bone sticking out from the back of Gibson's neck.

'It's Dan,' Franks informed the others.

'Is he dead, Ben?'

'Yeah, his neck's broke,' Franks answered. He turned to the body with the pitchfork sticking out of its chest. 'What the hell was old Spangler doing here?'

'Maybe they were trying to light out and leave us, Ben,' another of the gang suggested.

'Sounds like a mighty smart idea.' Franks rose to his feet. His face was drained of colour as he moved through the livery and out of the rear doorway into the pasture. The four younger men followed him closely.

'I don't like none of this, Ben.'

Franks glanced across at the outlaw.

'Neither do I.'

As the five men walked towards the fence-pole and the waiting saddles perched upon the top rails, they all sensed that someone was watching them.

Someone or something.

The fog seemed to float like myriad spectres across the large pasture where their forty horses waited. The chilling mist was obscuring the outlaws' view of everything around them and making Franks' younger men more than a little frightened.

As the five men stood shoulder to shoulder, beside the long fence-pole, each felt as if he had somehow entered a place where reality no longer reigned.

Franks dragged a saddle and bridle down and untied the long rope from its saddle horn. He started to unwind it.

'Take it easy, boys. All we got to do is just get these horses saddled up and ready for Hardin.'

His four men followed Franks' example and began to check out the horses around them.

As they all walked into the midst of the feisty horses with the ropes filling their sweating hands, they heard the noise of two guns being cocked in the shadows.

'I'd stop exactly where you are.' The chilling voice seemed to hang on the cold night air as the man wearing the bandanna over his face suddenly appeared through the mist beside the wall of the livery.

Ben Franks' eyes were first to spot the gleaming pistols in the hands of the masked man as he took in the words of warning. To the already weary outlaw, the sight of this ghostly apparition seemed only to confirm his gut-feeling that they were not fighting a human adversary at all, but something from another world.

A world where demons reigned supreme.

The fog grew thicker between Joe Smith and the five terrified outlaws. Dropping the cutting-rope to the ground, Franks drew both his weapons and fired. It seemed like an eternity before his companions realized what was happening and began firing as well.

As the drifting fog completely enveloped the pasture, the five outlaws started emptying their weapons in the direction where they had spotted the masked man.

The deafening sound of scores of bullets echoing around Powder Springs sent their forty mounts racing around the large grassy enclosure as the ruthless quintet edged forward through the dense mist.

When a sudden breeze cleared the fog and gunsmoke from the pasture the five men suddenly realized their target had disappeared.

'He's gone,' Franks gasped as he stared in disbelief to where Joe Smith had been standing only seconds earlier.

'What the hell was it, Ben?' one of the terror-stricken outlaws shouted as he tried desperately to reload his empty guns.

Ben Franks moved to the livery stable wall and gazed at the dozens of bullet holes embedded in it. Then he too emptied his guns of their spent shells and began fumbling bullets back into the chambers.

'It was a ghost, Ben. A real honest to goodness ghost, I tell you,' a shaking voice chipped up from behind the broad-shouldered Ben Franks.

'Did any of you boys see where he went?' Franks asked. He finished reloading his guns and stared anxiously about them as if trying to convince himself they had not been firing at a ghost but a human being. The darkness did not help to clarify things though; it only added to their irrational fears.

'No living man could have disappeared like that.'

'It was a ghost, I tell you.'

Franks looked around the pasture as he pondered the words of the young outlaw beside him.

'Take it easy, boys. There ain't no such thing as ghosts.'

'Then where did the critter go, Ben?'

Franks' eyes darted around the area trying to find a rational answer to the question. No matter how hard he tried, Franks could not explain to his men where the strange masked man had gone.

The mist began to swirl again, making it impossible see anything clearly.

'What the hell are we fighting, Ben?' another of the men shouted at him as he moved back to where he had dropped the long rope.

'Wish I knew,' Franks mumbled.

'Let's get back to the rest of the gang.'

'Come on, boys. Two of you start cutting out the

horses whilst the rest of us give you cover,' Franks whispered as he heard a noise coming from the street. 'He ain't coming back here in a hurry, I bet.'

Then the sound of tramping boots filled all five men's ears and they heard the creaking of the huge livery-stable doors.

'What's that noise, Ben?'

'He's by the stable doors, boys. Come on.' Franks cocked both his guns and signalled for the four men to follow him back inside the livery stable. Like obedient hounds, the quartet trailed Ben Franks as he ran inside the big dark building. Suddenly, through the dense fog, they saw spectral figures entering through the open stable doors.

'Look. The dry-gulchers!' Ben Franks exclaimed. 'Let 'em have it, boys.'

The sight of four figures raising their pistols as they spotted Franks and his boys rushing toward them started it. All five outlaws began to fan their gun-hammers. The interior of the livery soon filled with the choking stench of gunpowder as scores of lethal bullets tore across the vast empty stable in both directions.

Agonizing screams bounced of the wooden rafters as the red hot lead flew back and forth through the darkness.

As the smoke began to clear, Ben Franks found himself swaying. He realized he had been hit several times. He staggered towards the large open doors and began to laugh as he saw the bodies strewn out before him.

'We got the bastards, boys. We got them all.'

It was only when Franks reached the bodies that he looked behind him and saw that his four cohorts were lying dead. Ben Franks shook his head as he felt his warm blood pouring out from the three well-placed bullet holes in his midriff. He rubbed his sleeve over his mouth and stared at the crimson smear on his jacket.

As blood spurted from his wounds he gripped the wooden door to steady himself. Then Franks' burning eyes focused on the bodies before him.

These were not the masked man and his gang of bushwhackers lying in the dirt. There were four of the men who had been with Trent Hardin back in the saloon.

They had killed each other, he thought.

Like wet-nosed children, they had allowed their own infantile fears to overrule their years of experience and now they were all finished.

Pain tore through the outlaw as he felt his legs weaken and he found himself staring down at his own blood-soaked shirt-front as blood continued to squirt through the fine material.

Slumping to the ground, Franks felt the last drops of his precious blood gushing between his fingers as they tried vainly to stem its relentless flow.

There were too many bullet holes.

Sitting in the pool of glistening blood he felt the hairs on the nape of his neck start to rise.

Then Franks heard footsteps getting closer and closer behind him. The masked man was back and standing a mere six feet away from him, but it might as well been a thousand miles because he could no longer fight.

Only as he looked up at the masked face of the man known as Joe Smith did the dying outlaw work out what had happened here in the dark livery stable.

Hearing the gunshots he and his men had fired, trying to kill the man in the bandanna. Trent Hardin must have sent four of his men to help them.

Fear had caused both groups of men to see not what was truly before them, but only what they wished to see. Each group had thought they were finally facing the bushwhackers.

'Where the hell did you go when we started shooting at you out there?' Franks asked as the pain began to rip him apart.

'I just jumped behind the water-trough, Franks,' replied Smith.

'Damn, I never thought of looking there.' Franks spat blood at the ground as the figure loomed over him. 'Who the hell are you anyway, mister?'

Smith pulled his bandanna away from his face and allowed Franks to see his features. It had

139

been more than ten years since either man had set eyes upon the other, but it felt like only yesterday to both men.

After a few seconds, the outlaw began to laugh as blood poured from his mouth.

'You? But you're dead.'

'Nope, Franks. It ain't me who's dead, it's you.' Smith retied the dark bandanna over his face until only his eyes were visible.

Ben Franks started to blink when he saw the small Hoot Crawford appearing from out of the shadows. It was the last thing he would ever see.

EIGHTEEN

The ice-cold mist had completely filled the small community of wooden buildings and licked at the faces of five gunmen who stood in the centre of the main street. Trent Hardin and the motley four remaining members of his once mighty gang had not managed to complete this essential part of his bold plan: to drag women and children from their homes and tie them across the rail tracks.

The gun-battle had frozen each of them to the ground as they listened to the ear-splitting noises echoing all around them.

Hardin had never been a man to fear the unknown but the mist which choked the town and made it impossible to see more than a few yards was beginning to make him nervous.

How could he kill what he could not see?

The agony of not knowing what had happened was starting to get to Hardin as he stood amid the haunting fog beside his equally troubled men. As soon as he had heard the gunfire coming from the direction of the livery stable, he had hurriedly dispatched four of his best men to help Ben Franks and his small company of outlaws. For several minutes there had been silence, then there had been an even bigger gun battle, judging by the sound that had reached his ears as it rebounded off the walls of Powder Springs.

What had happened?

The leader of the once-powerful gang found waiting almost unbearable. Yet that was all he could do.

Hardin glanced at his last four outlaws and began to sense that these dim-witted creatures might be all that was left of his original troop. Each man clutched at his Winchester as they slowly stepped closer to their leader, who was holding his pair of Colt .45s firmly in his hands.

Terror seemed to dwell in the beads of sweat which rolled freely from every brow. They had good reason to be concerned: the town was now quiet again.

Too quiet.

Hardin turned on his heels, staring into the impenetrable white mist. From the centre of the main street, he could not see anything at all except the faint amber glowing of the closest street lanterns.

Swallowing hard, he concentrated on the pathetic men around him and wondered how he had managed to end up with four of the worst gunmen in his gang. Tom Woods was nearly fifty but had a brain which had ceased growing forty years earlier, Bo Leach was half Woods' age but no brighter or more capable. Cy Calhoon had been one of Spangler Brough's favourite cronies and had only ever been loyal to him. The fourth was another youngster named Johnny Snape who had once managed to kill three men in a fight, using a scattergun.

None of the four gave Hardin cause to feel easy in his mind. They walked across the street until they found a boardwalk and stepped up on to it. Staring up and down the street they all had the same view. A mere ten feet in any direction before everything dissolved into a white haze that no human eye could see through.

'Change of plan, boys,' said Hardin. He holstered both his guns and rubbed his face.

Woods leaned forward, holding his carbine across his middle.

'What ya mean, boss?'

'Before we can round up the women and kids, we had better try and find the rest of our boys,' Hardin answered. He led the four men slowly back along the boardwalk in the direction of the saloon.

'You figure any of them are still alive, boss?' Calhoun dared to question.

'Quit gabbing and follow,' snapped Hardin.

They stepped down from one boardwalk on to another at a different level. Their pace was slow and deliberate. None of the five was in anything which could remotely be described as a hurry.

For the first time since they had ridden into the remote town they could hear their own spurs jangling as they walked. It was an unnerving sound.

Each man knew that something lay in wait for them out there in the cold icy mist. Something so terrifying they could not even imagine what it was.

Hardin rested his hands on the grips of his guns as they walked ever onward towards their destiny. He knew his plan to rob the train was now over unless he could find another handful of his men alive somewhere in this small town.

Without added gun-powder, five men could not possibly take on the railroad guards.

He had to find Ben Franks and his men.

They had to be alive.

Hoot Crawford walked close to the tall masked figure of Joe Smith, acting as a human crutch for the wounded man. As they approached the bright saloon, Hoot knew they were now entering the mouth of a very dangerous enemy. Whether that enemy still had any teeth left remained to be seen.

The mist was thinner here than in the rest of Powder Springs as a stiff breeze swept up from the south along the rail track. Yet both men knew the mist was their friend and prayed it would not desert them completely as they stood in the shadows of the narrow alley.

Resting against the side wall of the saloon, the old livery man watched as Joe Smith found the last of his ammunition in his trousers pockets and filled the empty chambers of his two loyal Colts.

'We could have picked up a couple of the guns from them dead critters back at my stables, Joe,' Hoot suggested. He watched the tired eyes of his friend staring over the top of his bandanna at the limited view out in the foggy street.

'We only needed the carbine, Hoot,' Smith drawled.

'But what if you need to reload?'

Smith shook his head. 'I don't think I'll have time to load these guns once the shooting starts, Hoot.'

The alley was dark and free of the nerve tautening mist. Before them, the street and the rest of the town. Behind them, a twenty-yard walk to the iron tracks.

Smith looked at the Winchester in the old hands of the whiskered man and nodded.

'Twelve shots ought to be enough, Hoot.' His voice was weary and etched with the pain that burned from the wound on his side.

'But it's a gamble,' said Hoot. He sighed. 'I could have got you a hundred rounds off them bodies, if you'd have let me.'

Smith leaned on the wall.

'I figure if I can't finish them off with a dozen rounds, I don't deserve to live through this.'

It was clear to the old-timer that his tall friend was suffering far more than he would ever admit. Hoot placed a hand upon the brow of Joe Smith and could feel the heat pouring through the beads of perspiration.

'You got a fever, boy. You're burning up 'coz of that hole in your side. You ain't thinking straight no more,' said Hoot. He stared up into the glinting eyes.

'I'm OK, Hoot,' Smith reassured the older man.

Before Hoot could speak again he felt Smith's large hand on his chest as the masked man turned and looked along the misty street. He could hear them coming.

'Listen!'

'Spurs!' exclaimed Hoot Crawford. He moved closer to Smith his carbine in his hands. A weapon of which he had no experience.

'Yep. Spurs. They're coming, Hoot,' drawled Smith.

'Come on, son. You're hurt real bad and they're mean.' Hoot wanted to hide as he had always done when faced with danger.

'I've got to try and finish them.'

'Why you, Joe?'

'There ain't nobody else, Hoot. I'm the only chance this town has got. I can't quit.'

146

'But, Joe?'

Smith put a finger under the man's chin and closed his mouth to stop the flow of words.

'Remember what I told you. You have to get up on the saloon roof and draw their fire by shooting this rifle. I'll do the rest.' Smith's words calmed the older man.

Hoot Crawford could hear the spurs of Hardin and his remaining cohorts getting ever closer as he reluctantly peeled himself away from the wall.

'I ought to stay with you, Joe,' Hoot said quietly. 'You might need me.'

'I'll be safer if you're on the roof, Hoot. Get going.' The masked man shook his head and gently pushed the old-timer away in the direction of the track which led to the stairs and the roof.

'OK. OK.'

'Get yourself into position and remember to keep your damn head down. These varmints might just get lucky and part your hair right between your baby-blue eyes.' Joe Smith stood away from the wall and defied his own weariness.

Hoot touched the brim of his battered old hat and disappeared into the mixtures of darkness and fog.

Smith turned back to face the street and began to listen hard to the jingling of the rider's spurs as it hung on the dense ice-cold air. He cocked the hammer on one of his pistols until it locked into position, leaving the other weapon in its holster waiting for its turn to join in the action.

As he stared into the mist, Smith began to think about what he had instructed Hoot to do. The fever was making it hard for the tall man to concentrate but he could still recall telling Hoot to get on top of the saloon and hide behind the solid wood façade. From there he could start firing down into the street when he saw Hardin and his men returning.

Smith had two reasons for wanting Hoot to do this for him.

The first was that he needed the outlaws to be distracted and to waste ammunition while he got them in his sights.

The second and probably more personal reason was that Smith wanted Hoot Crawford as far away from him as possible when the showdown started. He knew the elderly stableman could not hit the sky with any accuracy but that did not matter, as long as he distracted Hardin and his cronies.

The masked man could no longer be certain of being able to protect himself, let alone the old-timer. On the roof, Hoot was at least reasonably safe.

As Smith edged closer to the corner of the saloon wall, he felt the wound on his side beginning to weep blood again. It was only a painful trickle at the moment, but the one-time bounty-hunter and lawman could not guarantee the wound would not open up again as it had done when Cole Dewer had originally blown a chunk of his ribcage off the side of his body.

Screwing up his eyes he could see faint images of the five figures across the wide street as they broke out of the thick fog and headed in the direction of the livery stable.

Sweat was running from beneath Smith's hat-band as he trained his gun on the blurred images opposite him.

He wondered, was it the shadowy mist or his vision which made the targets seem so distant?

Smith wondered why Hoot had not started shooting yet. Maybe he had not had enough time to get up on the roof.

Perhaps the old man could not see them.

A hundred frantic thoughts raced through Joe Smith's mind. Desperately he fought to remain focused as the burning flames of agony tore him apart. All his clothing was soaked in sweat, even though the night air was close to freezing in the streets of Powder Springs.

Then it happened.

A brilliant flame of rifle-fire tore across the street from above the saloon. The old man was shooting the Winchester wildly like all men did who had lived an entire life without ever having to resort to handling such lethal firearms.

Bullets bounced off the ground as the old hands

somehow managed to work the carbine's mechanism and pull the trigger.

Smith's ice-cold glare saw the five men taking cover as they tried to figure out where the shots were coming from.

Hardin seemed to be first to spot the rifle barrel as it protruded around the corner of a wooden façade high on the saloon roof.

Like the leader he was and had always been, Trent Hardin directed his men's fire up at the roof.

Cy Calhoun cocked his carbine and fired up at the rifle-barrel poking out from behind the façade. His first shot blasted the weapon from Hoot Crawford's bewildered hands, sending it tumbling down into the street.

'Got the critter,' Calhoun shouted.

Then it was the turn of the masked man.

From the dark shadows beside the saloon, Smith fanned his gun hammer three times and hit the jubilant Calhoun squarely in his inflated chest. The outlaw fell at the feet of Tom Woods who cocked and fired his Winchester twice in the direction of the man in the bandanna. The bullet which passed through Woods' belly sent him falling to his knees, shrieking. Smith's next bullet ended the high-pitched noise permanently.

Bo Lynch fired furiously at the saloon and tried to move closer to Hardin and Snape. As he too hit the ground, he seemed totally unaware his life had been brought to an abrupt end.

Hardin stared down at Lynch's glazed eyes before taking cover behind a water-trough as Johnny Snape stood defiantly firing his rifle at the dark shadows opposite them.

Holstering the empty gun, Smith drew the loaded one and started to cock its hammer.

It had taken too long.

The side of the wooden wall exploded into sawdust as Hardin emptied one of his own pistols in the direction of where he had seen the flashes of gunfire emanating.

Smith reeled around several times as his eyes filled with the burning splinters. Rubbing one eye until it cleared enough to see vague images, Smith returned a single shot.

Once again his aim had been true.

Johnny Snape, the last of Hardin's men, screamed and fell head first into the full water-trough. Water cascaded over the kneeling Hardin, soaking him to the bone.

'You OK, boy?' Hoot Crawford's voice called down from the saloon roof.

'Just keep your head down, old man!' Joe Smith shouted up. Feverishly he used his bandanna to rub the remainder of the agonizing grit from his eyes; then he heard the ringing of spurs echoing off the walls of the buildings.

Hardin was on the move.

True to his own hard-boiled image, the outlaw

was coming after him and not taking the easier option of trying to flee a town which had cost him so dearly.

Smith stayed on one knee, listening to the sound of the boots and spurs as they mounted the boardwalk twenty feet away from him.

A bullet blasted from Hardin's pistol as passed over Smith's Stetson.

Smith raised his weapon over the boardwalk and squeezed his trigger. He heard his bullet bounce off a distant wall. Another shot came from the lethal pistol of Hardin. This one was closer and made the kneeling man blink as its heat warmed the cheek of Smith's bandanna-covered face.

Smith moved closer to the wall and tried to see over the raised wooden boardwalk to get some idea where Hardin actually was. The light from the saloon flooded over the distance between them but made things no clearer.

For a fleeting moment, the masked man thought he had seen the figure of Hardin tucked in behind a large wooden bench placed beneath the glass saloon window.

Smith raised his gun and tried to get a clear shot at the man who was crouching a mere six yards away.

A blinding flash exploded from Smith's weapon as Hardin's bullet tore it from his hand and sent the startled man falling on to his back in shock.

As his spine crashed into the ground, he felt the pain ripping through him again. This time it was bad.

Really bad.

Smith stared at his hand as he lay on his back. All his fingers were still joined to his hand but they stung as if they had been attacked by a swarm of bees.

Before he could get up off the ground and search for his Colt, Smith heard Hardin's boots racing across the wooden boards towards him. Then the unmistakable figure loomed over him, bathed in the light from the saloon.

He looked like a demon as he hovered above the winded Smith.

Trent Hardin's gleaming gun was aimed straight down at Smith's heart.

'Pull down that bandanna, you bastard.'

Smith raised himself on one elbow and did as he was ordered. He could see the eyes of the man he had chased all those years ago beginning to recognize the image that faced him.

'You?' Hardin questioned.

'I guess maybe you know me at last, Hardin.' Smith managed to get himself into a sitting position as he stared down the barrel of the pistol.

'The bounty-hunter,' Hardin said as his memory began to answer all the questions he had bottled up inside him for so many hours.

'Yep, I was the bounty-hunter,' answered Smith.

He watched the man reaching out with the deadly pistol until it was aiming straight for his face.

'Laredo Layne.' Hardin mumbled the name bitterly. 'I thought you were dead.'

'It won't be long by the looks of it, Hardin.'

Suddenly the sound of a single shot echoed around the buildings of Powder Springs.

A single deadly shot.

FINALE

Hoot Crawford had scrambled down off the high saloon roof with the agility of a man half his age, and had headed along the dark alley at the side of the building until he reached the street.

With every nervous step, Hoot felt his heart pounding with anxious anticipation of what he might find once he reached the front of the saloon.

Hoot licked his lips, took a huge gulp of air and forced himself out between the buildings.

The sight which greeted him made him stop abruptly.

The scene was bathed in the light from the saloon windows and open doorway. It was not the sight he had expected.

Trent Hardin lay on his face, still holding his pistol in an outstretched hand. He was quite dead with a bullet-hole as big as a fist in the centre of his black-leather jacket. Blood and guts had spilled out from the body and dripped through the cracks in the planks of the boardwalk.

Cautiously, Hoot looked up from the gruesome sight and then saw the man he knew as Joe Smith stiffly leaning on a hitching rail. He moved to the side of the winded man.

'How did you do it?'

Smith said nothing as he turned his head and looked across at the bare-footed female who was holding the heavy pistol with both hands. Smoke trailed from its long barrel.

Ellie Vine was draped in the remnants of the clothing Hardin's men had torn from her body before they had used her. Somehow she had managed to prise the pistol from the hand of one of the dead outlaws and make her way through the misty streets.

She had remembered seeing Hardin kill Lucas Green outside the schoolhouse only minutes after the forty riders had arrived in town. When she saw him about to kill the man she knew had tried to help her, she had used the gun.

'Ellie got the drop on him?' Hoot whispered as Smith straightened up and began to walk toward the beautiful female slowly.

Smith did not reply as he reached the side of the dazed young woman. He carefully took the gun from her hands and tossed it away into the street before leading her inside the saloon and making her sit next to the warm stove.

Walking out from the saloon, Smith stepped back down next to the old man and toward his pistol in the alley. Hoot picked up the Colt and handed it to the taller man who inspected it before sliding it into his holster.

'Laredo Layne?' Hoot repeated the name he had had heard Hardin utter a few seconds before the gunshot. 'Is that your real name, Joe?'

Smith smiled. 'Nope. Folks used to call me that once but Joe Smith is a safer handle to live with, Hoot.'

'I reckon so,' the old timer nodded as he thought about it.

'I wonder why Hardin brought such a big gang to our little town in the first place?' Smith asked himself aloud.

'I guess we'll never know, Joe.'

'Reckon so.'

Suddenly both men heard the sound of a train whistle in the distance. It was the train heading north from the mint as it approached closer to Powder Springs.

'Must be almost three,' Hoot said.

Smith reached into his back pocket and pulled out the key to the rear door of his bakery.

'I'm going home to my family, Hoot,' Joe Smith sighed as he turned and began walking down the street and into the swirling mist.

'See you, Joe.' The old man watched the tall figure until he disappeared. Hoot Crawford knew nobody would ever see the masked gunfighter called Laredo Layne again.

Not unless trouble visited Powder Springs again, that was.